I0666373

Cleeve and Otis
Strike Again

First Edition

Published by The Nazca Plains Corporation
Las Vegas, Nevada
2009

ISBN: 978-1-934625-93-4

Published by

The Nazca Plains Corporation ®
4640 Paradise Rd, Suite 141
Las Vegas NV 89109-8000

PUBLISHER'S NOTE
Cleeve and Otis Strike Again is a work of fiction created wholly by *Christopher Trevor's* imagination. All characters are fictional and any resemblance to any persons living or deceased is purely by accident. No portion of this book reflects any real person or events.

Model Photo, Pomortzeff
Art Director, Blake Stephens

Dedication

This book is dedicated to my Author buddy Nicholas Bowman, for friendship, good advice and a wonderful imagination.

Cleeve and Otis
Strike Again

First Edition

Christopher Trevor

Contents

Introduction   1

Cleeve and Otis Strike Again   3

Captured Cop   13

The Marine   41

Justin Adams' Story   85

The Unseen Kidnappers   113

About the Author   151

Introduction

Since they were first introduced in "Greg Smith- The Times of My Life", a yet un-published book written by Christopher Trevor and since they have appeared in various books of Christopher Trevor's, the mysteries of Cleeve and Otis abound. Who are they? How is it they can get away with the things they do, kidnapping, tormenting and even raping their unwitting victims? How is it Cleeve can afford the mansion-like house he owns in the deserted area of what appears to be somewhere in upstate New York? Of course the stories that appear in this book all happened before Mr. Trevor's leather novel; "Love Torture and Redemption" saw the light of day. But for readers first meeting the maniacal Cleeve and his equally maniacal buddy, Otis, may I just say "Welcome" to a brutality and unrelenting sexcapade that you will not soon forget. The stories of Cleeve and Otis are sure to send a chill down many a reader's spine, specifically the male readers to be exact.

After reading Christopher Trevor's unsettling yet riveting new book, "Cleeve and Otis Strike Again", this reviewer is no longer sure where normal ends and abnormal begins. Take some of the characters that Mr. Trevor introduces us to in this collection of Cleeve and Otis tales, namely the men who fall victim to their wiles. We have Trevor

Don, a muscular long haired construction worker who finds the two serial kidnappers/rapists in the area he and his crew have been assigned to work on a recent construction project when he arrives for work in the early morning. Trevor becomes the latest of a line of construction workers that Cleeve and Otis seem to wallow in tormenting and working over in the lead story entitled the same as the book itself. In the story "Captured Cop" a handsome officer of the law is tricked into becoming a Cleeve and Otis victim. In "The Marine" a handsome serviceman and his fiancée are enjoying a summer evening out at in New York City at the Saint Gennaro festival. When the young marine excuses himself to relieve himself he becomes the latest of Cleeve and Otis' victims. And these are just a few of the characters that readers will encounter in this devilish collection of sadistic tales.

Cleeve and Otis, they are two men that are true sadists and twisted individuals, to put it bluntly. But are they really? Or is Cleeve just acting out all that he knows inwardly from another time in his life? And is Otis possibly along just for the ride? Whether this can be a case or not the two men prey on handsome unsuspecting men that they can torture, torment and rape for days. Once freed from Cleeve and Otis' clutches the victim is never the same…and neither will readers be the same after perusing this collection of thrilling tales…

Cleeve and Otis Strike Again

I had heard and read the police reports about Cleeve and Otis, those two man-hungry serial kidnappers and rapists. A buddy of mine is a police officer and I happened to be hanging out with him at headquarters one night before he got off desk duty and we went out to dinner. While waiting for him I saw the reports about Cleeve and Otis on my buddies' desk. I knew I wasn't supposed to be reading confidential documents but when something juicy is staring a guy in the face how can he resist? So, as I said, I knew about the men who quietly reported having been abducted, raped, and horribly worked over by Cleeve and Otis. Construction workers, businessmen, and military men seemed to be the two serial kidnappers' favorite types to go after. But I, never in a million years thought that *I* would become a victim to the two men's kinky and sexual antics. That night when my cop buddy and I went out to dinner I didn't mention to him how I had read some of the files he had left out on his desk about Cleeve and Otis. Maybe had I told him he would have told me that I had violated his files…OR maybe he would have told me how to avoid becoming one of Cleeve and Otis' man victims. My name is Trevor, Trevor Don to be exact. I work as a construction worker for Jim Green's construction company. I'm a supervisor and an on-site worker. I'm all of six feet tall, very muscular and well-toned from the work that I do plus the workouts that I punish myself through at the gym on a daily basis. I have wavy brown hair down to the back of my neck, a very thick mustache, and piercing blue eyes. The day that I want to tell you about my crew and I had been working on the eighth floor of an office building in Manhattan on Madison Avenue. We were renovating a bank vice president's office. I was wearing a black ribbed tight-fitting tank top, a pair of worn Levis blue jeans and black construction boots the morning that it happened. It was a Wednesday morning to be exact and I had arrived on the jobsite early to get things started, six AM on the dot. When I strutted into the office I was surprised to find the lights on because I distinctly remembered turning them off the night before. As I looked around the room curiously the door was suddenly slammed shut and my muscular upper arms were grabbed from behind.

"Got him Cleeve!!" the man named Otis shouted across the room.

"WH-what the fuck???" I stammered and began struggling in Otis' very strong grasp.

"I just love it when you fucking guys struggle," Otis said into my ear and nipped at my earlobe with his front teeth.

Cleeve sauntered over to us, a mocking grin on his face.

"Looks like another fine catch Otis my man," Cleeve said happily and tugged on the thin sleeves of my tank top.

"FUCK, I know who you guys are!!" I roared angrily.

"Good," Cleeve said. "Then we won't need to waste time introducing ourselves to you."

That said Cleeve ripped open the front of my tank top, exposing my hairy muscular chest and my two big pink nipples. Otis held me tight in a vise like grip as Cleeve gave my nipples a few hard squeezes and twists.

"ARRRGHHH!!!" I seethed through clenched teeth.

"Mmmm…nice tits," Cleeve mused.

I pushed myself back against Otis, Cleeve lost his grip on my nipples, and I kicked Cleeve hard, connecting directly with his balls.

"YOWWWRRRRR!!!" the bigger of the two men screamed in agony, grabbed his crotch and doubled over in agony.

"I am not those other pussy guys that you two sadistic faggots landed!!" I snarled, still struggling like crazy in Otis' grasp. "I will teach you two a lesson you won't soon forget! Come in here and grab me, tear my shirt??? Manhandle my tits??? We'll see about all that!"

"Fucking bastard," Cleeve grunted, still holding his crotch.

Otis tightened his grip on my arms and managed to hoist me a bit up off the floor.

"ULLPPP..." I gulped as my booted feet left the floor. "Strong fucker you are Otis boy..."

Before I could do anything more though Otis managed to lift me higher and he tossed me bodily over to a big pile of two by fours that my crew and I had piled up the night before. My head hit one of the pieces of wood hard, stunning the fuck out of me.

"Ohhh fuck..." I moaned miserably as Otis walked over to me.

He grabbed me by a handful of my long hair and yanked me roughly up to my knees.

"ARRRRGHHH..." I croaked.

"Find some goddamned rope to fucking tie him up with!!" Cleeve yelled angrily as he finally managed to straighten up.

Otis dragged me across the room by my hair as I screamed in a man's tortured pain. Moments later I was standing in the center of the room tied up and helpless. My arms were crossed in front of me and tightly roped together in three places, just under my huge pecs, levitating my sexy nipples, causing them to stick out nice and invitingly. My feet were also roped tightly together and worst of all, I was blindfolded with the red bandanna I had had in my back pocket. I stood there balanced on my tied up feet grunting and groaning as the two men sucked madly on my big nipples, running their mangy hands over my muscular arms at the same time.

"OHHH..." I moaned miserably. "Fucking tit hungry bastards..."

They squeezed my curled biceps hard, inflicting pain and then they began bighting down and really chewing on my poor nipples.

"ARRRRHHH!!!" I roared.

I had arrived at the jobsite at six AM. It was by now fifteen minutes past six. My crew would not be showing up till at least a little after nine AM. There was no chance of help for almost three hours. Man oh man was I in a fucking pickle of a situation. And I knew that Cleeve would most definitely be dishing out some form of revenge on me for having kicked him in the gonads. He and Otis chewed heartily on my nipples and sucked them so hard that I thought the two men were going to rip them right off my chest. Their hands roamed from my biceps to my chest area. As they continued sucking my nipples they ran their hands through the thick mat of hair all over my upper chest, pulling on it at the same time.

"OHHH... you fuckers!!" I seethed.

"I love it when they curse and swear like that don't you Otis?" Cleeve asked his buddy and then slurped my nipple back into his mouth.

Otis quickly agreed and also resumed sucking my nipple that he was working on. When the two men finally stopped sucking my nipples my nubs looked like two cherries stuck to my chest, that's how swollen they were.

"Man, his tits sure do look good and red sticking out from that hairy chest of his," Cleeve said to Otis.

"Yeah, they sure do," Otis said agreeably.

They then squeezed and twisted my sore nipples till I was again screaming in a man's agony. It actually felt like they were trying to draw blood from my nipples, but then they stopped torturing them. They tied rope around my upper arms, binding them to my chest.

"Fuck, you have to tie me up some more?" I ranted angrily, wobbling a bit on my tied up feet.

Cleeve and Otis laughed fiendishly as they roped my arms good and fucking tight. Then, they finished ripping my tank top off me and unbuttoned my jeans.

"Oh no, *no*," I blurted. "Please guys, no, no, I'm straight after all..."

"That doesn't bother us," Cleeve said. "We'll still milk the fuck out of you."

I stood there helplessly as the two men roughly pulled my jeans down to my knees, revealing the white pouch style boxer briefs I was wearing, and the hard-on I had in those boxer briefs.

"It never fails Cleeve," Otis said, running a hand over the big bulge in my underwear. "Right after they're tied the fuck up and worked over their dick always gets fucking hard. Even so called straight guys like this one..."

"Let's rip those goddamned jeans off him," Cleeve said with authority in his voice. "I want this muscle boy stripped to his underwear, boots and socks."

I managed to balance myself on my bound feet as they ripped and tore my jeans off me. I felt their hands now moving up and down my muscular tree-trunk like legs, squeezing my hard cock through my boxer briefs. Pre cum oozed and trickled out of my wide slit and stained my underwear. I felt Cleeve standing behind me. Suddenly, he whipped my blindfold off me.

"I really should make you pay for the kick you gave me in the nuts guy," he said to me, stroking my long hair in the back. "But I sure do admire a tough dude like you. And with what we have in store for you I'm sure that will be payment enough."

"You son of a bitch…" I seethed, facing forward as the guy played stroke with my long hair.

Otis, squatting in front of me reached into the opening in the front of my boxer briefs and pulled out my fat, hard cock along with my two big juicy balls. He quickly wrapped his lips around my manhood and began sucking it.

"OHHH…OHHH…" I moaned and rocked back and forth on my tightly bound feet.

Cleeve grabbed a handful of my long hair, yanked my head back, and kissed me roughly and meanly on the lips.

"MMMM…" Cleeve crooned as his tongue invaded my mouth. "MMMMM…"

Surprisingly, I found myself responding to Cleeve's kiss by forcing my own tongue into his mouth. Then, as Cleeve kissed me more and more I felt myself getting close to shooting my damned load. Otis was sucking my cock like his life depended on it.

"MMMM…" I also crooned.

Cleeve stopped kissing me and I looked down at Otis.

"Fuck man, *I'm going to cum, I'm going to fucking cum…*" I stated breathlessly. "OH you fucking guys, I'm going to shoot my damned load!!"

Otis sucked my cock into his throat and Cleeve squeezed my sexy ass through my boxer briefs as I shot my load a few seconds later.

"OHHH!!! YEAHHH!!!" I ranted and cried out loudly, my deep

voice filling the room. "FUCK YEAH!!!"

Otis gulped down every damned drop of my creamy sperm soup and Cleeve squeezed my ass cheeks harder and harder. It was as though he was trying to squeeze more of my slop out of my cock through my ass cheeks, GEEZ! When I was done spurting and squirting Otis let my cock slip out of his mouth and Cleeve let go of my ass. My cock went semi-soft and flopped against the outside of my boxer briefs.

"Feelin' good?" Cleeve asked me, rubbing my arms hard with the palms of his hands.

"Yeah, I suppose I do at that," I replied, catching my breath.

"Bet I know a way you could feel even better," Cleeve said mockingly.

With that Cleeve pulled my briefs down in the back, revealing my hairy butt cheeks. He gave them a few hard slaps and then he and Otis unzipped their jeans. I watched as they pulled out two of the biggest and meatiest boners anyone had ever seen.

"Oh no, no you guys…*please…*" I pleaded. "Suckin' my meat and torturing my tits was one thing, well that was two things, but please, not this…*not this…*"

"I'll get him ready Otis," Cleeve said and wrapped a huge muscular arm around my mid-section.

Cleeve lifted me up under his arm like I weighed nothing and carried me across the room and to a big workhorse that my crew and I used for cutting big pieces of wood.

"No, no, no…" I repeated over and over as Cleeve carried me.

In moments I was slumped over the workhorse and tightly tied down to the damned thing. My feet were untied and spread far apart, exposing my virgin, pink, asshole, and the red bandanna was now crammed in my mouth, effectively gagging me.

"RRRMMMFFFF!!!" I sputtered angrily, madly, and in total fear as Cleeve knelt behind me, licking my hole like crazy and squeezing my thighs.

My boxer briefs were off me by now and sticking out of the back pocket of Otis' jeans. I guessed that he intended to keep my damned underpants as a souvenir of this conquest. But my underpants were not my chief concern at that moment. Cleeve's tongue was lapping hungrily at my hole, flicking against the sides of it. He spit into my anal canal a few times and then sucked his saliva out of it, driving me batty, the feelings back there making my head spin. I could feel my most private region becoming super moist, good and lubed for the two men's big cranks. As Cleeve ate and licked and sucked my hole Otis busied himself tying rope around and around my mouth, really jamming the bandanna in place.

"There," Otis said, cupping my chin in his hand and looking at me. "When we fuck you you're going to scream soooo loud dude." I want to make sure you stay thoroughly gagged throughout your upcoming ordeal."

He let go of my chin and my head lolled forward. I was powerless, trapped, and totally unable to do anything to stop them. I was about to become one of the men in my police buddies' reports. Cleeve pressed his lips against my hole and sucked on it like mad. My head spun more and more and to my utter shock my cock grew hard between my legs. I felt Cleeve give my hard-on a squeeze from behind me and then he stood up.

"Okay Otis, he's wet as a used sponge back here," Cleeve announced, slapping his tongue against hips lips and eating the taste of my ass off them as he spoke. "Being that I got to eat his hole you can fuck him first."

"You don't have to tell me twice," Otis said happily and eagerly.

Otis stepped behind me with his huge boner in hand and pressed it against my sopping wet hole. As I said, I was about to become like those other guys I had read about in my police buddies' reports.

"RRRMMMFFFF..." I sputtered, looking back at Otis helplessly.

As the guy pushed his cock slowly into my hole it felt like his manhood was actually nibbling at me back there.

"OHHH yeah," Otis crooned. "Another damned virgin Cleeve."

"Not for long," Cleeve replied mockingly.

Otis' cock was halfway into my hole and already I felt like I was being stretched unmercifully.

"MMMFFFF!!!" I roared angrily, looking up at Cleeve now.

"Relax dude," Cleeve said and stroked my long hair.

Then, with a hard thrust Otis was all the way inside me.

"RRRRMMMMMMM!!!" I screamed in tortured agony.

Otis thrust in and out of my poor hole like a man possessed, slapping my ass cheeks hard at the same time.

"Fuckin' hairy butt cheeks this fucking guy has," Otis panted. "Maybe we should shave him after we're done here."

Cleeve laughed at that remark and Otis continued fucking the tar out of me like crazy and slapping my hairy butt cheeks. I sputtered angrily against my gag and struggled like a madman to get free. I vowed that I would kill Cleeve and Otis for this. If I had to spend the rest of my life hunting them down *I would get my revenge*. But then, my thoughts were cut short as Cleeve reached down and grabbed my hard cock tightly in his fist.

"RRRMMMFFF????" I sputtered yet again, looking at Cleeve with total rage in my eyes.

As Otis fucked my devirginized asshole Cleeve stroked my cock hard in his fist. I shook my head "no" back and forth till I was dizzy as hell, but when Otis shot his load, so did I.

"OHHH Yeah!!! YEAHHH!!!" Otis ranted like a madman as he shot his hefty-sized load into my hole.

I shot my second load into Cleeve's hand. He stroked and pulled every possible drop of my sperm soup out of my cock slit yet again. Let me just mention here that there is a real deep feeling of being violated for a guy when he's made to shoot his load, and he doesn't really want to at the given moment. When Otis and I were done creaming our loads he pulled his cock out of my hole and Cleeve licked my cum off his hand.

"MMMM…you taste good muscle boy," Cleeve whispered. "My turn to fuck you dude…"

Wasting no time whatsoever Cleeve stepped behind me and grabbed his hard whopper of a cock in hand.

"*MMMFFF…*" I said dismally.

As Cleeve plunged his monster-sized cock into my hole Otis squatted in front of me and greedily slurped my semi-hard cock into his mouth.

"RRRMMMFFFF!!!" I wailed as I was fucked and sucked at the same goddamned time.

I was sweating profusely; my mind was in turmoil, and I now knew how all those other men must have felt when Cleeve and Otis had used them this way. I again sputtered angrily into my gag, saliva spewing out of the sides of it.

"OHHH man, I'm getting close already dude," Cleeve panted as he speared me hard with his huge cock, slapping my hairy butt cheeks at the same time.

"MMMMMFFFF..." I wailed.

My cock was hard again in Otis' mouth. I felt the tip of his tongue probing my slit, forcing it in there. As Cleeve shot his load Otis sucked me till my cock felt numb and sore. I didn't cum a third time, but I felt Cleeve's cum as it filled my hole. It was warm, thick and soupy. When Cleeve pulled his cock out of my hole his cum dripped down the backs of my legs. Moments later the two men untied me from the workhorse, pulled the soggy gag out of my mouth, and retied my damned feet.

"You bastards!!!" I roared crazily. "What kind of madness is this???"

Then, I stood rigidly still in place and balanced on my bound feet as Cleeve and Otis took turns whipping my exposed ass cheeks with their leather belts.

"YOWWWRRRRR!!!" I roared angrily over and over. *"Damned fuckers..."*

As they whipped and whipped my ass my cock stayed hard as a rock in front of me, sticking out long and hard and painfully erect.

"Ha, ha, ha!!!" the two men cackled. "Whip that hairy ass, yeah, whip that damned hairy ass!!"

By the time they stopped my ass cheeks were red as a beet and I was whimpering like a child. Cleeve and Otis left me standing there crying and all tied up.

"Hey, fucking untie me you bastards!!" I yelled at them as they left the room, laughing. "*Shit!!!*"

When my first two workers showed up a while later I was utterly and completely fucking mortified to be found wearing just my construction boots and sweat socks, *and just as mortified to be found all roped up.*

"Good morning Trev---holy fucking shit!!!" Mike gasped as he walked in the door with Billy.

"Trevor, what the fuck happened here??" Billy asked as he and Mike came rushing over to me.

"It's a long fucking story guys," I replied angrily. "Two fucking guys busted in here and worked me over big fucking time..."

As I spoke Mike closed a hand around my sore cock and Billy ran his hands over my chest, squeezing my sore and very chewed up nipples.

"You know boss, you look real hot all roped up like this," Mike said, beginning to stroke my cock as Billy slurped one of my nipples into his mouth.

"*Fuck...*" I whispered.

Captured Cop

The two burly and overly rugged men were outside in the warm sun, thoroughly enjoying themselves in the back of the big house that the bigger of the men owned. The house was mansion-like, huge, situated by itself and surrounded by nothing but deep and dense woods. It was the only house on the long road that we had driven on for miles upon miles after they had captured me. Fucking fucks, but they had managed to capture me after I had pulled them over for driving way above the speed limit. Fucking totally fucks, nothing is worse for a cop than having the drop on him, worse if the perpetrator that gets the drop on you decides to kidnap your handsome ass. In my case two perpetrators had captured me, although when I had given chase to the speeding car I thought that there was only one guy in there, the driver obviously. That had been the huge mistake that got me captured, more on that soon. I have a long and miserable story to tell and I want all cops to hear it so that they don't make the same mistake I did. The bigger of the two guys was stretched out on a lounge chair in the warm sun as the other guy knelt submissively next to him, stroking his big cock for him. The two exceedingly muscular men were wearing nothing but jeans and construction boots, their huge beefy cocks and juicy balls sticking out of the fly openings of their jeans. Their rock-hard muscular bodies glistened in the sun, sweaty and smelling real raunchy and manly and the bigger guy squeezed and twisted the fuck out of his erect man-sized nipples as his buddy stroked his pre cum slicked cock for him. The submissive guy was quickly bringing the bigger guy to an impending gusher.

"Oh yeah, stroke my meat man, play with my damned skin flute," the bigger of the two men grunted, sounding breathless, his massive upper body arching itself slightly up off the lounge chair. "I'm getting close buddy, real fucking close now."

The guy kneeling submissively next to the lounge chair leaned down and slurped his buddies pulsing meat stick deep into his craw and began stroking himself as he sucked his foul mouthed crony like crazy.

"OHHH Yeah, fuck yeah, fucking A, that's it man, *that is the fucking ticket,*" the bigger man said throatily, squeezing and twisting the bejesus out of his own nips as he was now being sucked toward a gusher. "Suck my big meat man, suck the fuck outa me real good bud…"

He lay back on the lounge chair, his huge booted feet on the ground at the sides of the chair. His buddy slobbered messily over his big cock and quickly sucked it all back up, heartily sucking his bud's cock at the same time, stroking himself as well. It was a real raunchy and sexy free for all out there on that lounge chair. The guy kneeling on the ground was doing all the work, but obviously enjoying himself all the while. With the big guy's cock in his mouth he stroked himself with two hands; his cock was that big, his head bobbing up and down as he worked his erotic magic…

As for me, the poor cop telling this tirade, I was at the moment nearby the two men, struggling fruitlessly. Fuck, they had me locked in a wooden tool shed, my wrists cinched in my own damned handcuffs behind me and around a wooden post. How awful is that? How awful is it for a cop to be snagged and locked in his own handcuffs? My feet were securely tied to the bottom of the post with mounds of tightly wound white cotton rope around my ankles and just about up to my calves. I was clad in just my police issued lace-up black clonky shoes, my knee length black nylon socks (what the executives of the world nowadays refer to as OTC socks, OTC meaning over the calf) and my utility belt hung loosely around my waist, mocking the fucking shit out of me. My utility belt was minus my gun, my radio and my baton. My gun had been the first thing the two men had confiscated upon capturing me, obviously. My radio, my only contact to headquarters dispatch was with the two men, so they could keep an ear out for any rescue attempts that my cop brothers might be making on my behalf, their captured buddy. By the time headquarters dispatch had realized that I was in a shit-load of trouble I was long gone, kidnapped by the two men that I had planned on giving a ticket to for speeding. Without my radio on my person there was no way for my police brothers to contact me. My semi (fear) hard cock was twitching under my utility belt, dribbling beads of piss and slimy pre cum, humiliating! My succulent and hairy balls hung below my cock and utility belt like a damned chandelier. My uniform was thrown on a dusty chair at the other end of the tool shed. That was where they'd made me put it after forcing me (at gunpoint) to strip when they'd brought me to this godforsaken destination. How could this have befallen me I thought miserably as I struggled to what I knew would be no avail in my damned handcuffs. I had small hopes of perhaps knocking down the post I was trussed up to, getting my handcuffed wrists under my legs and end up bringing them in front of me. All of that before the two men outside the woodshed heard what the fuck was happening and snagged me again, *right!*

The post, unfortunately was embedded in the concrete floor of the shed and the top of it was supported by a ceiling beam, no chance whatsofuckingever of carrying out my little escape plan. And even if I did manage to get my cuffed wrists in front of me I didn't have my damned handcuff key. The two men had confiscated that as well, after my little escape stint back in the car, more on that later as well. My nametag and my badge I hate to have to admit to you where they'd pinned them for the time being, the time they were making me wait till they got around to round one of working me over. Okay, I'll tell you, my nametag was pinned to my left nipple, piercing it and my badge was pierced to my other nipple. God almighty, the pain when those two bastards had totally skewered my poor nipples I cannot even begin to describe it to you. And not before the two men had each slurped and sucked my big cop tits up to a state of erect and totally rigid. Fuck, never had any damned guys eating my man-sized cop tits before let me just state for the record. And now, now I still had no goddamned clue whatsofuckingever of what the two men planned to do with me, although I did have some pretty nasty and unthinkable ideas. I'm a cop after all and I know the fantasies that some sadistic faggots could have where a man in uniform is concerned. I mean, what the fuck else would two sadist faggots do to a cop once they'd captured him? My baton was laid across my uniform, also mocking me like my utility belt minus my gun and radio. I wondered dishearteningly if the two men planned to use it on me in different ways than they'd used it on me already. God, whacked and beaten with my own baton and cinched in my own handcuffs, what a fucked up turn of events that day! Leaning against the post in the wooden tool shed, my smooth muscular and bruised barrel-like chest and pecs jutting out all robust and sweaty I suddenly heard the sounds of the huge lug swearing in ecstasy as he shot his big load of creamy man's spunk.

"OHHH Yeah bud, that's it, fucking A again man, AAAAAAARRRRHHH yeah," the big dude grunted breathlessly, squeezing and twisting his nipples as his buddy stroked his mess from him. "OHHHRRRR yeah, fucking stud you are man!! Lookit this shit got me cumming like goddamned gangbusters here!!"

His massively muscled body was arched up on the lounge chair and listening to him from inside my woodshed prison I struggled even more to somehow get free, yet at the same time knowing it was no use. My handcuffs made jangling sounds as I pounded my cinched wrists against the back of the post. The oversized muscles in my upper arms flexed involuntarily and my biceps bulged real big with my fruitless efforts. Fuck, now that the big lug had shot his load it would be his buddies turn next. Then they would be coming in the shed to have some sinister and twisted fun with me, Police Officer Scott Reed, upstate New York City police officer to be exact. As I stood there in just my shoes, my socks and my utility belt with my semi hardness pointing straight out I thought back to how I had come to be in this most miserable of all predicaments, a predicament that no cop should ever find themselves in. As I thought about my dilemma I heard the sounds of slurping as the big guy gobbled his buddies' meat stick into his mouth... My semi hardness tingled between my legs in a mixture of fear and frustration of some kind. Beads of piss and droplets of pre cum oozed from my wide sexy cock slit...

"OHHH yeah, suck my muscle pipe now man, fuck yeah, we'll have a real sexy warm-up here and then we'll get to our handsome cop," the second guy grunted.

He now lay on the lounge chair squeezing and twisting his fat nipples while his big buddy suckled the fuck out of his cock.

As I said, my name is Scott Reed, Officer Scott Reed. I've been a New York City police officer now for the last three years, and damned proud of it too if I may say so myself. I'm twenty-four years old. I have thin black hair, cut real short, practically military style. The only other hair on my body is in my armpits and on my big luscious and succulent balls. I have intense dark eyes and at five feet nine inches tall my body is rock hard and well-toned from the daily workouts I put myself through at the gym nearly every night after I get off duty. Being that I live in Yonkers I'm stationed in the upstate area of New York City. On the day of my capture I was on a daily and routine patrolling. It was a muggy July afternoon and I thanked God that my police cruiser was air-conditioned. Dressed in my navy blue police uniform I was cruising along just under the speed limit on a lonely and deserted road in a woodsy area of upstate when seemingly out of nowhere a car sped past me, blowing exhaust fumes and grey smoke all over the road as it went, nearly side-swiping me by mere inches.

"HOLY FUCKING SHIT!!!" I roared and clenched my teeth in anger, realizing that the car had come up onto the road from the last entrance I had just passed on the lonely highway.

The roar of the car as it sped past me was deafening for a moment, startling the fucking fucks out of me, but being the good clear headed cop that I am I reacted instantly. I pushed the pedal nearly to the floor, turned on the overhead lights and siren, gripped the steering wheel with one hand and gave chase.

"FUCKING law breaker!!" I ranted angrily, reaching down with my other hand for my dispatch hand-held radio receiver. "Fucker nearly ran me off the goddamned road! Man, I am going to make sure this guy spends the next few weeks behind bars!"

I ranted and seethed all types of obscenities as I gained on the car before speaking into my hand-held radio transmitter.

"This is Reed, I am presently in pursuit of a speeding car on interstate two forty five," I said. "Come back."

"We roger that Reed," the female voice, a woman named Alma at dispatch replied. "What is the make and license plate of the car you are in pursuit of?"

"Looks to be a dark blue Monte Carlo," I replied as I sped along. "Can't say for sure, negative on the license plate at this time. The driver is speeding recklessly and so fast that the smoke from his exhaust and the road dust he's kicking up is blocking my view of the plate."

"How many suspects are in the car Reed?" the disembodied voice of Alma asked.

"Just the driver," I replied through clenched teeth as I sped faster still behind the car.

I put the radio down and coughing on the driver's exhaust smoke I signaled for him to pull over, the muscles in my arm burning with anger as I held it out my now rolled down car window. After a few more moments of chase the guy in the car finally slowed down. I did the same, killing the siren and flashing lights on the roof of my cruiser. I fleetingly thought how it seemed like he wanted to be caught, the way he had sped past a cop and all, but sadly I only thought that fleetingly, as I said. When the driver came to a full stop I grabbed the hand-held transmitter and switched it to microphone before speaking angrily into it.

"Stay in the car!" I spat irately. "I repeat, stay in the car!! Do not move and keep your hands on the steering wheel!!"

After issuing my orders I pulled my cruiser up a few feet from the car and slowly stepped out of my vehicle. I wasn't out of the cruiser more than three seconds or so and I was sweating in my short sleeved uniform shirt, the muscles in my arms bulging with anger in the sleeves. My police issued highly shined black shoes crunched on the pavement of the highway as I sidled up to the car, my hand near my holster. I noticed, but made no mention of it that the back trunk of the car was slightly open. I simply figured that that would just add to this guy's misery when I arrested him and gave him a ticket for speeding and endangering the life of a police officer. Had I been sharp enough to check that slightly opened trunk first before approaching the driver it might have saved me a lot of anguish. It might have prevented the two men from making off with me.

"Good afternoon Officer," the guy in the car said to me as he sat there with his big meaty looking hands on the steering wheel, the window rolled down on the driver's side, him glancing up at my nametag. "Reed, Officer Reed, *wow*, just like that old cop TV series back in the early seventies, Officer Reed, handsomest cop in TV land."

"Sir, may I please see your driver's license?" I asked the guy, ignoring what he'd just said in reference to my name, but God alone knew how many times I'd been teased and razzed about that by my cop brothers and buddies of mine. "And use your fingers only to reach for your wallet. I want your hands right where I can see them at all times!"

"Not to worry Officer Reed, I'm not armed," the guy said, obeying my orders.

"I did not ask you that Sir," I said sternly.

He got his wallet out of the back pocket of his jeans, took out his driver's license and handed it to me. I looked at it and saw that it was indeed a valid driver's license. The guy's first name was Otis but the last name had a smudge of some sort over it, obscuring it.

"Please step slowly out of the car," I said, taking a couple of steps back to give him ample room.

The door of the car opened with a loud creaking sound, masking the sound of the trunk of the car being slowly opened by the other guy who had been hiding himself in there. The guy named Otis stepped out of the car and stood before me in all his muscular glory. I could tell from the way his white tee shirt was pressing against his arms and chest that he was built like a brick shit house, his nips making two points against his shirt, it was that tight against his chest muscles. He was also wearing worn looking blue jeans and construction style worker mustard colored boots. I guessed his height to be about six feet and he had a dopey but sinister look about him.

"Did I do something wrong Officer Reed?" Otis asked me.

"Driving at nearly eighty miles an hour in a thirty-five mile an hour zone is most definitely doing something wrong I would say," I barked at him. "Not coming to a complete stop when you saw an officer of the law pursuing you is doing something wrong I would say. Endangering that officer's life by making him speed as well is doing something wrong I would say! Now, let's find out if you're under the influence."

I took another few steps back, my hands now held out in front of me, ready to catch the guy if he tottered, if he was at all intoxicated. I didn't know that taking my hand away from my holster was not the smartest thing to do at that moment. I also didn't know that with each step that I took backward I was walking back toward a shit load of trouble.

"Please walk a few straight steps toward me Sir!" I said

commandingly.

"I assure you Officer, I have not been drinking," Otis said to me, flashing a shit-eating grin.

"Just do as you're being told buddy," I replied sternly and watched as the big lug took a couple of straight steps.

Suddenly, from behind me I felt what felt like the muzzle of a gun pressed hard into my lower back.

"Not a move Officer Stupid," I heard a husky sounding voice say from behind me. "And keep *your hands* right where *I* can see them!"

I instantly froze in terror and my eyes opened wide in shock at this sudden turn of the tables.

"*Son of a bitch,*" I muttered through my clenched teeth.

Now I knew why the trunk of the car had been slightly opened. Fuck, the other dude had been crouched down in there the entire time. This was looking more and more like an evil plan to snag a cop.

"Now, slowly, raise your hands, you know the way I'm sure," the voice from behind me said with total confidence, pressing what felt like the muzzle of the gun harder into my lower back.

I gulped hard and reluctantly and sadly moved my hands and arms straight up in the shape of two letters "L."

"Good boy Officer Stupid," the guy behind me said and still pressing what felt like the muzzle of a gun into my lower back confiscated the gun in my holster.

I felt a twang of pain in my heart as my gun was taken from me. Otis was standing in front of me grinning sadistically from ear to ear at my peril.

"Y-you guys are making this real difficult on yourselves," I said through trembling lips as the guy behind me sidled up next to me, my gun in his hand, in his other hand a sawed off broom handle. "Fuck, it wasn't a gun you had pressed into my back man, *you weren't even armed!!*"

"No, but I sure as shit am now," the guy with my gun in hand said meanly. "And besides, I did you a favor Officer Stupid. I didn't bash you over your handsome head with that broom handle!"

Grinning as sadistically as Otis the handsome muscular hunk tossed the sawed off broom handle under my police cruiser. I gulped again and sick at heart now realized how I had been so awfully had. In total anguish I slowly curled my hands into loose fists, preparing to make my move.

"Looks like a good catch as usual Otis," the bigger of the two guys said. "Never thought that we would land such a handsome officer of the law, but as the saying goes, what the fuck?"

He was dressed just as Otis was, in worn looking jeans, a tight tee shirt and mustard colored construction boots.

"L-look man, give me my goddamned gun, you're making a big mistake here," I said to the big lug as he stepped back behind me, my gun held in his hand pointing at my back. "You boys won't get away with this shit! Harassing a police officer is against the law!!"

I curled my raised hands into tight fists, keeping that look of terror on my face, my chest jutted out. If I was to make a move they needed to think I was terrified. At my last remark the two men started laughing, telling me how they were going to do a lot more than just harass me.

"I told you he would pursue me if I sped past him Cleeve," Otis said to his big buddy. "I've seen this handsome piece of cop ass patrolling this area for the last few days now."

Fuck, had they been stalking me??? Now I knew for sure that this was a plan to snag a cop.

"I knew he would make a good mark for us," Otis went on, reaching for the baton on my utility belt.

Fuck, fucking fuck, *they were* planning on kidnapping my handsome ass! I seethed inwardly in a mixture of terror and anger, no fucking way I was going to allow this to happen, not without a confrontation at least! As Otis helped himself to my baton I pursed my lips tightly together. One of the mugs had my gun and now the other one was taking my baton, fuck, I was being stripped of my arsenal one piece at a time, but I *was ready*. I whirled around as fast as possible and swung a hard clenched fist at Cleeve's face, hell bent on getting my gun back from him. Fucking fucks, I was prepared to kill both of these guys if it came down to that! But Cleeve was fast, and from what I witnessed he'd been dutifully trained in armed combat. As I whirled around, as I threw out my fist he took a few quick steps back from me, causing me to miss my intended target.

"HUFFFFF!!!" I grunted angrily as the big lug pivoted out of my way and my tightly clenched fist hit nothing but air.

As my fist missed Cleeve's jaw he raised my gun, pointed it at my face and pulled the trigger. The sound of the gun only clicking, seeing as the safety was on nearly startled me out of my shoes. The sound of the clicking of my gun a second time as Cleeve tormented me seemed to fill the air around us and from behind me Otis whacked the back of my knees with my baton, hard.

"UHHHNNNNFFFFFF!!!" I grunted at the sudden pain, the lower part of my legs and calves feeling like they had been turned to jelly.

Cleeve took a step toward me, my gun pointed at my gut. I saw that the safety was now off the weapon and Cleeve's finger was slowly pulling the trigger back. My hands instantly flew straight back up, palms open this time, real vulnerable feeling as I wobbled unbalanced in my aching jelly-like legs.

"D-don't man, *don't shoot me!!*" I gasped. "*Please man...*"

"Got a wife and kids copper?" Cleeve asked me mockingly, clicking the hammer back on my gun, his calling me copper making him sound like a villain out of an old-time movie. "That's the line all you pigs give when you're in a shit-load of trouble!"

From behind me Otis Whacked the back of my upper thighs harder than hard with my baton and at that moment Cleeve rammed me a good hard punch to the old gut, totally knocking the wind out of me.

"HOOOFFFFF!!!" I sputtered and doubled over in pain, my uniform hat falling off my head and landing on the ground.

The pain behind my knees and in my upper thighs was immense. I straightened halfway up and turned slowly to face Otis, a scowl of outright hatred etched on my face. But as I turned Otis rapped me hard across the side of my knees with my baton and then I heard a gunshot fill the air.

"HARRRRRRRRRRRRRRR FUCK!!!" I roared in total and sheer terror now, turning and seeing Cleeve holding my gun pointed at me, the scent of gunpowder filling the air.

Despite the pain I was in I snapped quickly to a stance of near attention and raised my hands high. I stood before the two men gasping for air, my breath coming short, feeling like I would piss in my uniform pants. My knees and thighs were hurting real bad but for the purposes of my life I managed to stay up on my feet. I was sopped in fear sweat and embarrassingly to say my meat stick was fear hard in my uniform pants.

My eyes darted wildly back and forth in real terror anger and frustration as the two men seemed to be looking me over lustfully. I was starting to realize exactly why they had been stalking me and why they had ambushed me.

"Officer Reed, come in, Officer Reed, please respond," my radio suddenly squawked on my utility belt.

"Ha, if headquarters could see you now Officer Stupid," Cleeve said, holding my gun pointed at my chest as Otis next took my radio off my belt.

Fuck, fuck, double and triple fucks, I felt like a knight slowly being stripped of his armor. I grimaced miserably as Otis turned my radio off and held it up.

"We'd better get moving Cleeve," Otis said. "No doubt this pig alerted his dispatch when he started pursuing me."

"Yeah, the only thing we want his cop buddies finding when they get here is his abandoned cruiser," Cleeve said.

"You guys are going to pay for this shit!!" I seethed; as I faced Cleeve.

"We don't plan on paying for anything Officer Stupid," Cleeve said to me with a mean looking leer on his face, the muzzle of my gun pressed against my bellybutton. "Not when we can get it for free with you."

Again the two men chortled loud and mockingly. I gulped hard as Cleeve took a few steps back from me, still holding my gun pointed at me as Otis next took my handcuffs off my belt.

"Okay Officer Stupid, you're going to take a ride with us," Cleeve said and then my heart thundered in mortal terror. "A long ride to be exact…"

I stood rooted to the spot, my mind in a tailspin as Otis did the honors of locking my wrists behind me, in my own damned handcuffs. With my gun in Cleeve's hand still pointed at me I felt it best at that moment to do as the two men wanted…my time would come soon…I hoped…

"Okay Otis, blindfold this pig and lets get on our way," Cleeve said, stepping over to their car and opening the back trunk.

"Y-you're planning on putting me in the trunk of your car?" I stammered in total fear as Otis tied a white cloth over my eyes, effectively blindfolding me.

"Heh, if it was good enough for me while you were pursuing us then it'll be good enough for you Officer Stupid," Cleeve laughed.

Every time they called me "Officer Stupid" I seethed with red blinding fury.

Holding me by my upper arm Otis guided me over to their car and the two men hoisted me roughly into the trunk. They curled my legs back to force me to fit and I admit I was shuddering in total fear by then. What had just happened to me is every cop's worst nightmare.

"Let's get going," Cleeve said and I heard the trunk slam shut. "I got a feeling his cop buddies are on the way. I can smell pig in the air."

I shuddered more than in terror as the two men climbed into the car and sped off, the only evidence that I had been there were my police cruiser, the broom handle under my cruiser that Cleeve had used to trick me with, and my uniform hat on the ground where Cleeve and Otis had left it.

It was about ten minutes or so into that ride that I started to think somewhat coherently. So far we had been driving straight on the road, which meant that we were still on the interstate where I had begun my pursuit of the speeding car. As I continued to think coherently I also recalled the fact that like any good cop I didn't keep my handcuff key on my utility belt, rather, I kept it in the back pocket of my uniform pants. Smiling behind the blindfold I slowly wriggled my hand into the left-hand side back pocket of my uniform pants...

As I reached for my key I felt the car turning off the interstate, no way now of knowing where the fuck they were taking me.

I got my fingers around the key and managed to slowly pull it from my pocket, being super careful not to jostle myself in the confines of the trunk. I didn't want the two guys knowing what I was up to until I had the advantage, entirely...

I managed to make my hands and fingers stop trembling long enough to get my handcuff key out of my back pocket. Then, using my sense of feeling and touch I methodically worked the key into the tiny hole of the cuff on my right wrist. I held my breath and gave the key a turn. I exhaled with a sigh of relief, only wishing that I had my radio on my person so that I could signal my fellow officers. I was sure that by then my cop brothers had found my abandoned cruiser on the road. No doubt a search would ensue and be out in full force for the missing officer. But until some kind of help arrived I was essentially on my own. I slipped the key back into my pants pocket...

The car came to a halt more than an hour or so later. By then my legs and arms were feeling pretty numb and awfully cramped from having been restricted for so long. I wondered in horror where they had brought me. I also wondered what my chances for escape were without my baton or gun. Fucking fuck, but I had to try.

"Well here we are Cop, home sweet fucking home at last," I heard Cleeve saying as the two men got out of the car, slamming the doors.

I kept my freed hands behind me, not yet wanting the two men knowing that I had slipped out of my handcuffs. The trunk of the car was pulled open and I felt their hands grabbing my upper arms, hoisting me roughly out of the hot trunk. I came out all sweaty. Once I was on my feet I was prepared to make my move.

"Hope you enjoyed the ride Copper," Cleeve said, straightening my necktie as he spoke. "And if you didn't enjoy the ride, well, we don't give a flying fuck!"

His hand was on my tie and I didn't feel my gun pressing into my back. It was time to make my move... It was now or never...

I quickly reached up, yanked the blindfold down and away from my eyes and landed a good hard punch to Cleeve's jaw, sending him sprawling to the ground.

"HOOOOFFF!!!" Cleeve grunted as he hit the ground. *"Fuck, the pig is free Otis, how the fuck???"*

As I had punched Cleeve my back was turned to Otis. As I turned to pummel him next he beat me to the punch. Otis still had my baton in hand and he used it most skillfully. Like at the time of my capture he rapped me good and fucking hard behind the backs of my knees. Actually, this time he rapped me about a hundred times harder than he had at the time of my capture.

"HARRRRRR!!!" I roared in the blinding pain and fell to the ground on my knees.

As I tried to quickly stand up Otis rapped me again, good and fucking hard this time across my chest with my baton.

"UUUHHHNNNFFFFFF!!!" I grunted and found myself sprawled on my stomach this time, flat on the ground.

I did not even recall turning and landing on my front side after Otis had so meanly rapped my pecs.

"OHHH GAWD," I groaned miserably, pressing my palms flat against the ground.

"How in the fuck did he get himself free???" Otis asked Cleeve angrily. "Those handcuffs were locked tight around his goddamned wrists! I made sure of it."

Squatting over me, my gun in his hand pointed at my back Cleeve reached into the back pocket of my uniform pants. Like a child who's just won an award Cleeve held up the handcuff key. Jeez, it seemed like the punch I had given Cleeve hadn't even winded the fucking guy.

"This is how he got free," Cleeve said calmly, yet the awful trace of sadism in his voice rang through loud and fucking clear.

Then, grabbing me by the collar of my uniform shirt Cleeve hauled me roughly and meanly to my feet.

"ACCCHHH!!!" I barked the front sections of my shirt and tie pressing hard against my Adam's apple, choking me, the tips of my shoes dangling above the ground as Cleeve hauled me up higher by my shirt collar. "F-fucking bastards!!"

When I was flat on my feet again I quickly took in the sight of the huge mansion-like house sprawled out all by itself on the lonely road.

"WH-what is this place you've brought me to?" I asked, still gasping for air as Cleeve held me by the back of the collar of my uniform shirt.

Before receiving a reply to my question though Otis rapped me again good and fucking hard across my pecs with my baton.

"HUUUFFFFFFF!!!" I seethed in pain and clenched my teeth in agony as Cleeve held me up by my shirt collar. "UUUUURRRHHH!!!"

I felt like I was going to choke on my blood if Otis rapped me again that way...

My handcuffs were still dangling off my left wrist, seeing as I had only freed my right wrist while in the trunk.

"This place is my home Officer Stupid," Cleeve said directly into my ear, his tongue grazing and his lips teasing my lobe. "I own everything you see in front of you."

"WH-who are you man? Who the fuck are you?" I whimpered as the two men began hustling me toward the huge house.

"Heh, that's what everyone wants to know," Cleeve responded mockingly. "Come on Otis; let's put him in the woodshed for now. I want to have some warm-up fun before we get to work our new acquisition over..."

"Son of a fucking bitch..." I muttered under my breath as the two men walked me to the back part of the huge house, each of them holding me tightly by one of my arms pulled painfully behind me.

I walked in a wobbly fashion, my knees and thighs aching awfully from the blows they had been dealt, my poor pecs stinging with searing pain as well. When I saw the woodshed where they planned to keep me I struggled mightily, somehow having found a second wind.

"F-FUCKERS!!" I garbled crazily, kicking my legs out as I was moved along. "This is kidnapping!!! And kidnapping a police officer is a federal offense!"

"Yeah, that it is for sure Officer Stupid," Cleeve laughed and the two men hoisted me a few inches off the ground.

They carried me as I continued struggling, my legs kicking out even more-so now as they brought me into the woodshed. Once in the shed the two men tossed me bodily against the wooden post that I would soon be trussed to.

"HUUUFFFFF!!!" I grunted in pain anew as my upper torso connected hard with the post.

I quickly wrapped my arms around the post to keep from falling, my handcuffs dangling mockingly from my wrist. Looking around the woodshed as I turned to face my captors I knew then and there that I was in a shit-load of trouble. These guys were not planning on letting me go anytime soon.

"Okay Cop, start stripping," Cleeve said with total authority in his voice as he and Otis stood a few feet away from me, Cleeve holding my gun pointed directly at me. "Down to your shoes and socks..."

I gulped hard and held up a trembling finger.

"N-now look man, kidnapping me is one thing, hauling me into the trunk of your car was downright monstrous and beating on me is going to cost you big fucking time eventually," I said through quivering lips, trying to sound as authoritative as possible and not as terrified as I was actually feeling. "But there is no fucking way that I am going to strip my uniform off for you two perverts!!"

I concluded my tirade by spitting on the floor…

With his teeth clenched Cleeve raised my gun, pulled the trigger and the shot was deafening in the small enclosure of the woodshed. I felt the bullet whiz past my head and pass through the small window of the shed, just about missing me.

"*Shit, shit!!!*" I screamed in bloody terror and threw my hands up. "TH-this shit is against the law man!! You're terrorizing a cop here!!"

Still holding the gun pointed at me Cleeve pulled slowly back on the trigger. I nearly shit my uniform pants when I saw that the muzzle of the gun was aimed directly between my eyes. I grabbed at my necktie with a quaking hand.

"Strip now Officer Stupid!!" Cleeve said meanly. "Or the next shot you hear will be the last."

"My cop brothers will get you guys for this!" I whimpered angrily as I undid my necktie.

"The question moreover is will they get you?" Otis asked me with a grin as I unbuttoned my uniform shirt.

I shucked off my sweat sopped uniform shirt, revealing my bruised and overly muscular barrel-like chest. The two men looked at me lustfully and gesturing with my gun Cleeve pointed at the dusty chair a few feet from where I was standing.

"Take your nameplate and badge off your shirt, hand them to Otis and place your shirt and tie on that chair," Cleeve ordered. "Then get your pants and under shorts off."

With my hands trembling I did as I was told and sadly handed Otis my badge and nametag. Then, I stepped over to the chair and neatly placed my shirt and tie on it. I undid my utility belt and regular belt, placed my utility belt on the chair and facing the two men who had captured me dropped my uniform pants down around my ankles, revealing the fact that I was wearing no under shorts.

"Ha, looks like we got us a freeballing cop," Cleeve laughed. "No under shorts to keep as a souvenir this time Otis."

My cock was rock hard with fear, betraying me and my big juicy plum-like balls hung low in my sexy sac…

Without a word, and feeling totally humiliated I bent over to get my uniform pants off over my socks and shoes. I could feel my two captors taking in the sight of my smooth tight bubble shaped butt cheeks and my pink bunghole while I was at the task of getting my pants off.

Cleeve and Otis were licking their lips as I stood straight up and practically at attention before them when I was stripped to my police issued lace-ups and my long black dress socks. The two men watched with total satisfaction as I placed my pants on the dusty chair along with my shirt and tie.

"Put on your utility belt Cop," Cleeve said to me, the hammer on my gun cocked back.

Doing as the man said I picked up my useless utility belt, slipped it around my naked waist and pre cum oozed and dribbled from my slit, betraying me some more. I breathed heavily...

"Now, get yourself situated against the post over there, back pressed against it, hands behind you and wrapped around it," Cleeve ordered, my gun pointed now at my head.

"Look, stop this now, *please,*" I said softly, standing there in my almost total nakedness.

Cleeve squeezed the trigger of my gun and without another word I hastily dashed over to the post and positioned myself as he had told me to. My heart felt beyond heavy as Otis did the honors of relocking my wrists behind me, again in my own handcuffs, this time around the post. Cleeve mockingly held my handcuff key.

"Want to try to escape again Officer Stupid?" Cleeve asked me.

I simply pursed my lips together as Otis stepped next to me, looked at me lustfully and grabbed a handful of my big low hanging balls, squeezing them hard.

"AYYYYRRRRRRRR!!!" I seethed in a man's pain through clenched teeth. "Fuck man, easy with my balls!!"

Chuckling, Otis let go of my low hangers and squatted in front of me to get busy roping my feet to the bottom of the post. He used white cotton rope that had been piled near the post, securing my ankles good and tight, practically up to my calves. He toyed with my long socks, snapping the elastic in them against my skin as he did his work. A few times he stole glances at my pre cum oozing cock...

"Tie him good and fucking tight Otis," Cleeve said. "Officer Stupid isn't going anywhere for some time."

I looked at Cleeve across the woodshed, utter misery showing in my eyes.

When I was tied and cuffed securely to the post Cleeve put my gun down on the chair where my uniform was along with my baton.

The two men stood at my sides, looking me over, really drinking in the sight of the conquered officer of the law.

"Real good catch Otis," Cleeve said, sounding real proud of his buddy. "As always…"

As always? I wondered what the hell that comment meant. Had these two men done this sort of thing before? Had they kidnapped other cops and terrorized them the way they were doing to me, or worse? I wondered if there were reports somewhere in police files on Cleeve and Otis. Somehow I had to find out, but for the moment I had more pressing issues it would seem. The two men began running their mangy hands all over my torso, roughly rubbing my chest, squeezing my nipples hard and twisting the very fucks out of them. They reached behind me to grab handfuls of my muscular tight butt cheeks. I literally seethed.

"Fucking perverts!! Get your dirty hands off me you mugs!!" I grunted at them.

"Ha, you are not in any goddamned position to be telling us what the fuck to do Officer Stupid," Cleeve laughed and gave one of my big man breasts a hard squeezed jiggle, following that up with a hard open handed resounding slap.

"OWWW!!! Fuck!!!" I spat angrily. "Bad enough you beat on my pecs with my baton, but now you need to be slapping the fucks out of them too?"

While the two men were kneading and mauling me I'm sad to say that my cock was hard and twitching between my tree-trunks like legs, my balls churning from the squeeze Otis had given them a few moments before…

Looking down, I watched in horror and with my mouth hanging agape as the two men leaned down over my big fleshy man-sized tits and slurped one of them each into their mouths. The sounds of sucking and slurping filled the air in the woodshed as my captors feasted on my man tits.

"AAAAAARRRRRHHH fuck, fucking fucks, no, no, no you guys, I'm no goddamned faggot!" I ranted. "Fucking fuckers, don't be treating my cop tits like a buffet!"

Ignoring me, Cleeve and Otis sucked harder on my tits, nipping at them with their front-most teeth, pulling at the sensitive tips of them with their lips and teeth, seeing how far they could stretch them out on my massive chest. I writhed against the post as chills of agony and ecstasy consumed me, my crotch area jutting out provocatively. My cock was hard and oozing and dribbling small droplets of my cop pre cum.

"FUCKERS, I am going to fuck you mugs up for this!!" I croaked miserably, looking up at the ceiling of the woodshed, not wanting to watch as Cleeve and Otis worked the fuck out of my man tits.

By the time the two men stopped it was a good (bad?) fifteen to twenty tit torturing minutes later. And…by the time they stopped my man tits were worked up to the size of two ripe cherries jutting out on my chest.

Fucking fucks, by the time the two men stopped my tits were feeling beyond sore, beyond sensitive. GOD, by the time they stopped…

What they did next was unforgivable and should not ever happen to any cop…

"Give me his badge Otis," Cleeve said.

"WH-what are you mugs up to now?" I seethed as my teeth clenched again. "Don't be fucking with my badge man! That's a cop's prized possession! A cop's badge shows that he's made it!!"

"Oh yeah, you made it alright Officer Stupid, you really made it," Cleeve laughed.

But as I ranted on and on about the merits of a cop's badge Cleeve pulled back the pin on it, tweaked my right-sided nipple up to a swollen nub and pinned my badge right onto said nipple, skewering it.

"AYYYYYRRRRRRRRRRRR!!!" I screamed in bloody agony, looking down at the sudden pain and immense pressure in my poor man tit. "OHHH FUUUUUCCCKKKKK man, *Ohhh GOD, no!!! YOU bastard!!!*"

The two men looked gleefully with eyes filled with sadism as a thin line of blood trickled down my chest from my newly pierced nipple.

"OHHHRRRR you bastard!! L-look at what the fuck you did to my poor nipple man!! You mutilated it!!" I screamed in Cleeve's face.

"Otis, you may have the honors of doing his nameplate," Cleeve said.

With my eyes still opened wide in terror I turned my head to look at Otis… He was holding my nametag in his hand, the pin on the back of it pulled open.

"You ready Officer Reed?" Otis asked me and grabbed my left-sided nipple in his thumb and first finger.

"OHHH no, no man please," I pleaded as Otis tweaked my left-sided nipple up into a swollen nub, rolling it in his finger and thumb, just as Cleeve had done to my right-sided one.

I squeezed my eyes shut tight in utter agony and felt the mean pinch as my nametag skewered my left nipple.

"AAAYYYYRRRRR!!!" I screamed again in total agony, the sound of my voice filling the woodshed.

Tears streamed from eyes a few seconds later as the two men took turns squeezing my hard cock and yanking and twisting my low hangers.

"Y-you sick bastards are going to get more than a couple of years behind bars for this shit!!" I ranted in pain, the pressure on my nipples immeasurable to say the least.

"Oh, I doubt that very much Officer Stupid," Cleeve said mockingly. "Seeing as you or your cop buddies have no fucking idea where you are. HA!!!"

Looking down again I now saw that there were now two thin lines of blood trickling down my muscular chest.

The two men let go of my cock and balls and looked me over for a few seconds. The woodshed was hot as hell and I was a sweaty and grunting mess at that point. Stripped to my shoes and socks and wearing my useless utility belt, my nametag and badge pinned to my damned tits and cinched up in my own handcuffs; fucking fucks, what a sight for a cop of my caliber I thought miserably.

My cock twitched long and fear hard between my legs...

"Come on Otis, lets go relax outside in the sun while Officer Stupid here gets used to his situation," Cleeve said, giving one of my big man breasts a mean hard jiggle.

"Sure thing Cleeve," Otis said, giving my other man breast a hard resounding slap.

"OWWW!!!" I barked, watching as the two men exited the woodshed, closing and locking the door behind them.

"*Fuckers, perverts,*" I whispered through clenched teeth.

I didn't bother yelling for help, seeing as there was no one around for miles to yell for help from...

So there you have it, there you have the sad narrative of how I came to wind up in this God-awful predicament.

Then, my thoughts of my capture and early tortures were cut short as I heard Otis grunting outside that he was now shooting his load. Fuck, the two men would be coming for me at that point. I just knew it.

"OHHH yeah, fucking awesome Cleeve," Otis groaned outside in the sun as Cleeve stroked and choked his mess from him, Otis' cum landing all over his massively muscular chest. "Feels great man!!"

Otis' mess of cum on his chest glistened on his chest in the sun as Cleeve lovingly licked it up, swallowing and gulping it in greedy mouthfuls. Cleeve was paying special attention to his buddies' nipples as he ate the cum off them.

"OHHH ea-easy with my tits Cleeve," Otis panted in the afterglow. "You know how fucking sensitive a guy's tits are after he shoots his goddamned big hefty load."

"Sure as shit Otis my man," Cleeve said agreeably. "And you can imagine how the cop's tits must be feeling at this point."

When all the cum had been licked off Otis' chest the two men sat side by side on the lounge chair, Otis holding my police radio in hand. He flicked it on and the two men listened.

"Yeah, this is Officer Johnson calling dispatch," they heard through the static, seeing as we were obviously out of transmits range. "We've recovered Reed's cruiser and his uniform hat. But no sign of the officer anywhere."

"We roger that Johnson," the female voice of Alma at dispatch responded. "We'll put out an APB of Officer Scott Reed. All units in the immediate area to be on the lookout for him."

Otis turned off my radio and the two men laughed heartily and sadistically.

"Immediate area!!" Cleeve's voice boomed. "Immediate fucking area? Fuck, they have no goddamned clue just how far out of the immediate area their brother cop is!! Fucking Officer Stupid!! Come on Otis!!"

A few seconds later my heart thundered as the woodshed door was opened from the outside. The two men stood in the archway in all their muscular glory, clad now in just their thick white sweat socks and construction boots. They each had cocks of the meaty and jumbo size; Cleeve's being the meatier, longer and fatter of the two. Their low hanging balls looked like they were bulging and chock filled to overflowing with their man juices. Fuck and they had each shot hefty loads. It looked like these two sadists could go all day and then some... A thin trickle of after jizz dribbled from Cleeve's cock.

"You ready for us Cop?" Cleeve asked as he and Otis entered the woodshed in a predatory-like manner.

"Ready for what???" I asked them angrily. "Are you two perverts ready to let me go at this point? You heard my buddy Officer Johnson on the radio. My cop brothers are out there searching for me at this very moment."

"Sure as shit they are," Cleeve said as he and Otis sidled up to my sides, jiggling my nametag and badge on my poor tortured man tits, sending chills of searing pain through me. "But I seriously doubt that they'll be coming here looking for you...and in a woodshed at that. HA!!!"

"OWWWRRRRRR!!!" I grunted and arched my crotch area forward; my hard as a flagpole cock swinging outward as the two men pulled and tugged on my nametag and badge, causing indescribable pain to shoot through the thin skin of my cop tits. "Don't you two bet on it! When a cop is missing his cop brothers and sisters will search fucking high and low till he's found...OWWW SHHHIIIITTTT!!!"

"This cop cock of yours got hard waiting for us?" Otis asked me mockingly, reaching down and giving my low hangers a tight squeeze and my hard cock a twirl, sending droplets of my pre cum splattering to the floor.

"I fucking doubt that," I seethed in the man's face and involuntarily gyrated my crotch area, the way I was being handled attested to that sexy movement I supposed. "As I told you mugs, I'm no damned faggot!!"

Smiling meanly Otis slowly slid to his knees in front of me, wrapped his hands around the top-most part of my long black socks and slurped my hard crusted cock into his mouth.

"OHHH oh no, oh no, not this you perverts," I seethed in a mixture of ecstasy and outright humiliation. "OH GAWD, don't be sucking my cock man!!"

Standing beside me Cleeve took my badge in hand and undid the pin skewering my nipple that it was hanging on.

"WH-what are you doing man?" I asked him through trembling

lips.

Slowly, Cleeve slid my badge off my nipple, the pain coursing through my nub sending waves of pain through my very being.

"AAAYYYRRRRRRR fuck, my poor tits!!" I seethed with tears in my eyes.

Looking down as Cleeve got my badge off my nipple I watched in utter disbelief as Otis sucked my crusty hardness for all he was worth, giving my low hanging sweaty balls a few tugs and squeezes every few seconds.

"OHHH GAWD, GAWD, GAWD of GAWDS, I do not fucking believe this you mugs, but I'm getting close here," I panted madly, arching my crotch area sexily forward. "I'm going to shoot a real cop-sized load of spunk here you bastards!! Fuck, got me sweatin' in my socks!!"

Droplets of blood oozed to the tip of my nipple that Cleeve had just taken my badge off of. I blanched and nearly passed out when he sucked my bleeding nipple into his mouth and chowed the fuck on it.

"OHHHRRRRRR fuck, wh-what are you, some kind of blood sucking vampire pervert?" I asked the guy, but then my words were cut short as I felt myself shooting my load, right into Otis' mouth, right down his stinking gullet. "ARRRRHHH sssshiiiiiiiiitttt, lookit this shit, fucking cop kidnappers got me cummin' like goddamned gangbusters!!!"

I balled my cuffed hands into a tight fist and sweating like crazy arched my head back against the post. Otis went on and on sucking the fuck out of my manhood, gulping down my mess each time I erupted, siphoning me.

"OHHHRRRRRR p-perverts, eating my cum and sucking the blood from my damned tit," I seethed.

Otis' tongue was like magic as it swirled around my spurting cock. I again arched my crotch area forward, looked down, saw how my cock was impaled in Otis' mouth and let fly with another good strand of my good stuff.

"UHHH..." I grunted as Otis scoffed down that eruption as well.

When I could not cum anymore Otis got to his feet and standing beside me took my nametag in hand. Cleeve stopped sucking my bloody tit momentarily and watched as Otis did with my nametag what he had done just moments before with my badge. Otis undid the pin holding my nametag to my pierced tit and slowly slid the needle off it.

"AAAYYYRRRRRRRR fuuuccccckkkkkkk!!!" I screeched throatily.

"Like I said Cleeve, a guy's tits are always sensitive after he shoots a good-sized load," Otis said.

"Sure as shit," Cleeve replied and took my low hangers in hand, squeezing them. "And from the way these balls of his are feeling all hefty he's going to be beyond sensitized by the time we get done with him today..."

The two men chuckled meanly; they both leaned down then over my chest and greedily slurped one of my bleeding tits each into their mouths.

The sounds of my agony mixed with forced ecstasy filled the small woodshed and the scent of sweat and cum assaulted my nostrils as the two men ate my cop tits with utter gusto. It was a horrid feeling as they sucked and chewed on my nubs and I felt the blood oozing from them. I swear it was like a psycho nursing baby was on my goddamned tits.

Later, Cleeve and Otis exited the woodshed a second time, leaving me handcuffed and roped at the feet to the post still, this time blindfolded as well...

"We'll be back again real soon Officer Stupid," Cleeve called out to me from the door of the woodshed. I heard the door of the shed pulled closed and locked. I silently thanked God that they hadn't pinned my nametag and badge back to my poor swollen and wounded cop tits.

"Come on Otis, lets let Officer Reed get his energy back," I heard Cleeve saying. "In the meantime we'll check on that slave of ours down in the shaving room..."

My mouth dropped open in outright horror at what I had just heard Cleeve say... A slave in a shaving room???

What had I fallen into here???

Who was Cleeve? Who was Otis? What the fucking fuck was to become of me???

I leaned the back of my head against the post and cried big tears of fear behind my cloth blindfold...

Author's After-word:

The short story "Captured Cop" was inspired by various factors. It amazes me how such a short story could have so many influences and inspirations…

Originally the story was dedicated to a past AOL buddy of mine named Scott. Scott had a severe fetish for wearing his business suits to work with no underpants on underneath his suit trousers. The word for this particular fetish is "Freeballing." It was because of Scott that I named the captured police officer in the story "Scott." (The reason for the cop's last name being "Reed" will be explained in detail shortly.) It was also because of Scott and his request that when the cop in the story is stripped down to his socks and shoes that it be revealed that he is not wearing any underpants, that he is "Freeballing" in his uniform, as Scott had so aptly stated it. Over the years I lost contact with Scott but the story will live on…

To sum it up the story chronicles in very quick detail a police officer's worst nightmare, of being abducted by not just one but two crazed lunatics, and in this case who better than my two crazed recurring characters, Cleeve and Otis…

Cleeve and Otis made their first appearance in a segment of my fictional memoir, "Greg Smith- The Times of my Life." At the time of that writing Cleeve and Otis were meant to be only support characters in that particular story. But as time went on I decided to give Cleeve and Otis their own series of stories. They were so villainous in their appearance in the "Greg Smith" story that I felt they deserved more recognition. I also felt that readers of my work could get some good insights into just what these two unique characters were capable of… It also gave readers a peek into my darker side of writing as well… It was determined in "Greg Smith- The Times of my Life" that these two rugged and brawny men were always on the prowl in the wee morning hours for what they both called "male marks" that they could use for their sadistic antics. In the Cleeve and Otis stories that I went on to write it was revealed that after they abducted and worked over their latest "male mark", the man was released within twenty-four hours time of his abduction, usually. Greg Smith was an exception, seeing as he was, in Cleeve's words, "something to really hold onto." In "Captured Cop" Cleeve and Otis hold onto the cop and at the story's end it is never determined when they will release him...if at all... Cleeve's mention of the slave they have in their shaving room is a direct (and yes, deliberate) plug to my story, "Larry, Captured by Cleeve and Otis." This story, "Captured Cop", is also one of the rarities where we see Cleeve and Otis being affectionate to each other in a sexual sense. This surprised me, especially as the author, seeing as Cleeve and Otis always maintain that they are straight and that the only reason they hunt and capture men is that men fight and resist a lot better than women do. It is also the first story where Cleeve uses a gun to terrorize a mark. In this case he uses the captured cop's confiscated service revolver. This story shows a rawer, more primal side of Cleeve.

The character of Officer Scott Reed in the story "Captured Cop" was largely and nearly directly influenced by Officer Jim Reed (although the cop's first name of Scott as I mentioned was because of my AOL buddy Scott) from the 1970's TV cop series, "Adam-12", who was portrayed to perfection by actor Kent McCord... (If you're wondering why I named the leather master "Kent" in my story "Love Torture and Redemption" now you know.) As my artist buddy Joe T. once said "Officer Jim Reed was the handsomest cop ever in TV history. In the episode of "Adam-12", entitled "Trouble at the Bank", Officer Jim Reed is taken hostage by two bank robbers when he unwittingly walks into a robbery-in-process. One of the men who capture Officer Reed is named Cleeve, although in the TV episode his name is spelled "Cleave." When I first saw that episode years ago the name "Cleeve" stuck in my head for whatever the reason, perhaps because it seemed to be a very uncommon name. Perhaps also, it just sounds like a name for a really mean guy, no offense to any guys out there named Cleeve. Or maybe I somehow knew that I would be using the name for a fictional character of my own at some point down the line...

The opening scene of "Captured Cop" where Officer Scott Reed is cinched to the post in the woodshed while Cleeve and Otis are outside enjoying themselves in the sun I admit I lifted directly from the Zeus video "Ranch Slave Trainee." In that video's opening sexy Canadian porn actor and lanky muscle boy Jimmy Dean (no, not that Jimmy Dean) is seen tied to a post in a woodshed, his hands cinched behind him and his booted feet cinched to the bottom of the post, keeping him balanced and in place. The tied up actor is clad in no more than his boots and a pair of ripped up denim short shorts with his cock and balls dangling out the side of them. While Jimmy Dean struggles to get untied and swears under his breath over his bondage plight, his two captors porn actors James DeFalco and Mark Saber (I believe those were the actors in that video) are outside in the sun enjoying each other sexually. I decided on Cleeve and Otis to be the kidnappers in my story "Captured Cop" rather than two new characters when I saw the Zeus video. The reason for Cleeve and Otis' affection toward each other for the first time is explained in the opening scenes of the Zeus video, seeing as I very much wanted to mirror that. Even the way Officer Scott Reed struggles to get free mirrors Jimmy Dean's gyrations in the video. Like James DeFalco and Mark Saber in the video Cleeve and Otis are extremely muscular, very sadistic, yet very attractive men. In the video "Ranch Slave Trainee" it is never explained how Jimmy Dean came to be tied up in the woodshed. If one ponders it long enough it could be that his two captors nabbed him when he was hitchhiking. It is possible that he could even be a captured police officer of some kind, like in my story. Jimmy Dean saying, "You gonna let me go or what?" as James DeFalco and Mark Saber enter the woodshed explains that he has been captured and is an unwilling mark in their sadistic game of sexual torture…

At some point down the line I will more than likely write a sequel or two for "Captured Cop", but for the moment I think it stands pretty well on its own…

Happy Reading…

-Christopher Trevor-

The Marine

"Hah!! Ever seen a marine in such a fucked up yet hot position?" the man named Cleeve asked his buddy Otis gleefully.

"Shit Cleeve, I never saw such a hot looking fucking marine till now, let alone seeing him in the position he's in," Otis chortled. "I'm really glad we decided to snag this guy when we saw him at the feast with that girlfriend of his."

"Yeah," Cleeve laughed meanly. "I wonder where the fuck she is now, probably thinking that this hot young marine of hers ran off on her with some other piece of female ass. Instead, what she's thinking is the farthest thing from her mind that happened, because we got her hot marine all trussed up in a really fucked up and hot position."

They had me atop a table, stripped to my white torn up briefs and my black knee length dress socks. My uniform, which they had stripped off me earlier, was strewn all over the floor of their hotel room. Seeing my uniform strewn all over the floor that way sent a feeling of utter shame through me. A marine's uniform is something he takes pride in wearing, because it's not just any guy that can wear that uniform. Being a marine had always been my dream and I had worked hard for the honor of wearing that uniform, and now these two bastards had stripped it off me and threw it all over the floor like rubbish. The position that I was in that they were talking about was pretty miserable and damned uncomfortable to say the least. I was hog-tied on that damned table, roped like a caught steer. My hands and muscular arms were pulled stiffly behind me and roped to my socked feet at the ankles that were pulled up behind me to meet my hands, my legs bent back and my knees up off the table. A good amount of rope was tied tightly around my mid-section just above my ass and around the table, binding me tightly to the table I was hog-tied atop of. A wad of duct tape was pressed over my mouth, thoroughly gagging me. My hole was feeling pretty wet and lousy, seeing as the two bastards that had snagged me had just spent the last two hours or so taking turns fucking the tar out of me before hogtying me. Fuck man that has to be the most horrible thing to happen to a guy let alone a marine of my caliber. Every time they dicked me in the ass I felt a mixture of shame, rage, and pain coursing through me. My ass cheeks were feeling pretty lousy as well. Actually, my buns were feeling like they were on fire, seeing as they had spanked the fuck out of me with a variety of things up to and including wooden paddles with holes drilled in the damned things. Shitty thing to have happened to a marine let me tell you, to have his asshole fucked repeatedly as if he were some whore. Actually, my hole had been turned into a sloppy, cum slicked cunt after having been repeatedly fucked by the two men. They had gleefully shot load after fucking load of their hot thick spunk into me, filling my hole with it. I rubbed my ass cheeks together and a chill coursed through me as it felt all moist and slicked up back there. My dick, a rope tied around the base of my nuts twitched long and hard under me, sticking through the hole that was cut in the table I was hog tied atop of. Droplets of pre cum oozed out of the tip of my hard pulsing sausage thick meat and landed on the floor.

"RRRmmmfff…" I sputtered angrily, looking wildly at the two men with utter hatred in my eyes, thinking what a horrible twist of fate this was for a United States marine.

I had been on leave in New York City, I had been at the Saint Gennaro feast with my beautiful girlfriend when these two bastards managed to snag me and spirit my ass off to their damned hotel room…

My name is Mark Sommers, Corporal Mark Sommers to be exact. I am a United States Marine and damned fucking proud of it if I do say so myself. I'm twenty four years old, I have severely buzz-cut blond hair, crystal blue eyes, and my hairless body is well muscled and much toned from the workouts and physical training the marines put us through on a daily fucking basis. I am originally from Florida, I am stationed in Georgia, and to celebrate my promotion to Corporal I was spending a week in New York City with my girlfriend, her name is Laura. I met Laura in Georgia during my first year as a marine private and we have been together ever since, three years to be exact. I plan to marry Laura, after I am honorably discharged from the marines in another year. She has long brown hair, dark eyes, and the softest skin I ever had the honor of trailing my fingers over. The moment I first saw her at the jazz club that my buddies and I were hanging out in on that Saturday night three years ago my breath caught in my throat. Two of my marine buddies and I had a Saturday night pass and we had decided to go to an old fashioned jazz club. We were sitting at a table a few feet away from where Laura and two of her girlfriends were sitting. While the singer was performing on stage we kept stealing glances at each other, smiling at each other in a friendly and warm way. When the singer on the stage invited all couples to come out onto the dance floor before singing a slow jazz ballad I decided to take a chance. I gulped hard, placed my half-empty mug of beer on the table, and stood up. My buddies watched as I made my way over to Laura's table. Dressed in my olive colored dress uniform, complete with shirt and tie and patent lather lace-up marine issue shoes I walked over to Laura's table. I took my flap hat off, leaned over a little, and politely asked Laura if she would do me the honor of dancing with me. She looked at her girlfriends and they all smiled from ear to ear. She said she would be glad to dance with me. Needless to say my heart was pounding wildly in my chest. I folded my hat over my belt, took Laura by the hand, and led her out onto the dance floor. I could feel my buddy's eyes on us and I was sure that Laura felt her girlfriend's eyes on us as well.

"I'm Mark," I said to her, not able to take my eyes off her beautiful face.

"I'm Laura," she replied. "You're a marine."

"Now how did you know that?" I asked her with a grin.

"Oh, I read minds, and the uniform sort of gave it away," she said with a smile as we found a spot on the dance floor.

I put an arm around her waist and took one of her small slender hands in mine. As we danced slowly I could not help pulling her close to me. She was easily the most beautiful woman that I had ever set my eyes upon. Her other hand found it's way to the back of my big neck and she rested the palm of it there, gently caressing it with the tips of her fingers, sending chills through me.

"So, where are you stationed Mark?" she asked me softly, looking adoringly into my eyes.

"Here, in Georgia," I replied breathlessly. "I'm originally from Florida."

"How many years are you signed up for?" she asked me.

"Four," I said.

As we danced we looked intently into each other's eyes. She glanced at my nametag and looked up at me again.

"Sommers," she said. "What rank goes before that?"

"Private," I said, smiled, and blushed. "I just joined up six months ago. This is actually the first Saturday night that my buddies and I over there have been out on in that long. I never thought I would have the pleasure of meeting such a beautiful girl, let alone having the pleasure of dancing with her."

She smiled at me and pressed her hand harder against the back of my neck.

"Laura, may I buy you a drink after this dance, and then perhaps we could have dinner some time soon," I said to her hopefully.

"I would like that," she replied and gave me a quick kiss on the cheek.

My heart thundered in my chest…

So, after that night I dated Laura on a pretty much regular basis. I always stayed on my best behavior on the base, never giving my commanding officer any reason whatsoever to not give me a Saturday night pass out on the town. Laura is a year older than I and lives alone in a one-bedroom apartment. The first time we made love it was the sweetest, most wonderful experience of my life. I stood at attention with a white cloth blindfold tied over my eyes as Laura slowly undressed me, taking my uniform off me piece by piece. I smiled from ear to ear as I felt her fingertips moving over my hairless muscular chest.

"Why the blindfold?" I asked her mischievously, feeling my big dick getting super hard in my uniform pants.

"You'll see in a few minutes," she replied and ran the tip of a finger over one of my big pink and very pointy nipples.

I shuddered as I stood there rigidly at attention, her fingers teasing me and driving me crazy. When I felt her hand moving over my swollen and pulsing crotch I gasped, sucking in a big mouthful of air.

"Oh Laura," I whispered breathlessly as she slid my belt off me.

She unbuttoned my uniform pants and they slid down my legs, bunching up at my ankles, revealing my white briefs, along with the big pulsing bulge I was sporting in them. Laura put an arm across my shoulders and held me balanced as I stepped out of my uniform pants over my shoes and socks.

"I love you Mark," she whispered and held my face in her hands as she planted two delicate kisses on my trembling lips. "From the moment I saw you I knew I loved you, my handsome and noble marine. When I was sitting there in that club with my two girlfriends I couldn't take my eyes off you. I confess that I prayed you would ask me to dance."

She kissed me again as I stood there in just my briefs, shoes, and socks, and the blindfold still tied over my eyes.

"Oh Laura, I love you too," I whispered and reached out for her.

Teasing me, she stepped away from me.

"You can take off the blindfold now Mark," she said.

I reached up and pulled the blindfold down from my eyes, leaving it dangling from my neck. I saw Laura standing before me in a see through black silk negligee, a pair of high heeled black pumps, and black silk stockings with garters on them. Seeing her that way made my breath catch in my throat and my dick oozed pre cum through my white briefs. In the dimly lit room her eyes looked hungrily at my crotch.

"Oh God Laura, no wonder you blindfolded me," I said with a wicked grin on my face as I stepped over to her.

I grabbed her tightly and clamped my mouth down hard on hers.

"Make love to me Private Sommers," Laura whispered in my ear, her hands behind my neck, stroking it.

She kissed the side of my neck and I lifted her into my strong muscular arms.

I carried her over to the bed. As I held her over the bed she kicked her shoes off and then I laid her gently down on the satin sheets. I leaned down, unlaced my shoes, pulled them off my feet, shucked my briefs off, and wearing just my black dress socks and the blindfold dangling around my neck I slid onto the bed next to her. My marine sized dick was hard, pulsing, and standing at attention, just like a real marine. I trailed my fingers over the silk see through negligee she was wearing till my hand rested on one of her nipples. I squeezed it gently and she pulled my head toward it. As I took her nipple between my lips my heart swelled with love for this woman, as did my hard and pulsing dick. She placed a hand behind my neck and stroked it gently as I sucked at her nipple. She made small moaning sounds and at that moment I was so very glad she was the first and would be the only woman that I would ever want in this way. Unfortunately for me though Laura would not be the only person I made love to in my life. No, all that changed the night her and I were in New York City celebrating my promotion to corporal and also celebrating our third year together...because that was the night that those two bastards, Cleeve and Otis abducted me and turned me into their personal fuck slave...

It was a warm September evening in New York City that night. Laura and I were staying in an inexpensive hotel on Thirty Third Street just off Seventh Avenue and we had ridden the train downtown to Little Italy to enjoy the Saint Gennaro feast. We ate sausage and pepper hero sandwiches, pastries from an Italian bakery, and sipped frosty pina coladas as we walked the crowded streets of Little Italy. The scent of sausage and peppers and other foods being cooked right out on the sidewalks filled the air. Dressed in my olive colored dress uniform, complete with size eleven highly spit shined patent leather lace-up shoes and a corporal's hat (no longer a private's flap hat) I walked proudly with Laura hand holding onto my arm. I had a corporal's stripe on my uniform jacket sleeve. We were very much in love and totally oblivious to everything around us, especially to the two men that had been trailing us as we moved through the feast. When we came upon a wheel game where you could win a stuffed animal I saw the look in Laura's eyes and we walked over to the booth. Instead of numbers there were names on the board in front of us. Without a word I pulled two dollars from my wallet, placed one dollar on the name Laura and the other dollar on the name Mark. Other people around us placed their dollars on their name choices and then the girl in the booth spun the wheel.

"It's going to stop on your name," Laura said as she stood in front of me with my arms around her.

I kissed the side of her neck and said, "You're wrong, it's going to stop on your name."

With the lights of the feast shining in her eyes Laura watched as the wheel slowed down, and then, sure enough, it stopped on my name.

"Well I'll be damned," I whispered in her ear, smiling proudly.

"Mark!!" the girl in the booth shouted and Laura let out a gleeful sounding whoop.

She chose a green stuffed dog and held it against my chest.

"The color almost matches your uniform you handsome devil," Laura said to me and kissed me on the lips.

"Congratulations Soldier," I heard a very husky sounding voice say to us.

I glanced to my side and saw a big construction worker type guy standing there, along with another construction worker a little shorter than he was. They seemed to be looking at me intently.

"He's a marine, not a soldier," Laura said proudly, and in front of the two men kissed me on the lips again.

"Even better," the shorter man said and they walked on.

Little did I know that the next time I saw them I would be trapped in their hotel room and at their mercy.

Laura and I walked on in the other direction from the two men. I didn't tell Laura but a chill had crept up my spine when I saw the way those two men were looking at me, practically drinking me in with their eyes. As Laura and I were passing by an Italian restaurant I realized that the need to piss had set in pretty strong. Seeing that the restaurant wasn't all that busy I told Laura I was going to dash in there and see if they wouldn't mind if I used their facilities.

"I'll wait here," Laura said as we stood in front of the restaurant.

I had no idea whatsoever at that moment that I would not be seeing my beautiful Laura again till the next day, the next evening actually... Leaving Laura standing there with her stuffed dog I trotted into the restaurant. A waiter approached me and asked in an Italian accent if he could help me.

"May I use the men's room?" I asked him politely, practically snapping to attention out of force of habit.

"Of course sir," the waiter replied, noting my uniform. "Go through the second dining room all the way to the back, turn left, it is the door on the right."

"Thank you much," I said and walked quickly in the direction he had indicated.

There were a few patrons in the front eating area but the second dining room was empty. Looked like most people were eating outside at the feast I thought as my dick pounded piss hard in my uniform pants. I found the men's room and dashed in. Standing over a urinal I unzipped my pants, pulled my big thick beefy and very erect dick out of the fly opening, and held it in my fingers as I pissed a long marine sized load into the urinal.

"Ahhh, better," I whispered as relief filled me and my piss filled the urinal.

When I was done I flushed, and as I was about to pack my softening dick back into my pants it happened. From behind me I was clubbed viciously over the head with what felt like a metal pipe.

"Uhhhnnnfff..." I gasped.

My uniform hat took a good amount of the blow but I was still knocked into a stupor. I fell to the floor in front of the urinal I had just pissed into, my dick still hanging out of my pants and my hat on the floor of the bathroom. I felt myself being lifted and then hoisted across a big burly shoulder. I was carried out of the men's room like a sack of potatoes over that big burly shoulder.

"Take his hat Otis," I heard a familiar sounding voice say. "We'll take this hot looking marine out the back way. No chance of anyone seeing us that way..."

At that point I totally blacked out...

The first thing I realized when I came to a while later was that my hands were securely roped behind me at the wrists. I came to on the floor of a seedy looking hotel room. I managed to pull myself to my knees and look around the room.

"Wh-where the fuck am I?" I asked groggily as my vision adjusted to my surroundings.

The room was musty smelling, with an orange carpet that had a lot of cigarette burns in it. The walls were four different shades of paneling, a large king sized bed dominated the center of the room, and a table was at the side of the bed. It was the table that I would eventually find myself hogtied atop of when the two men started milking the fuck out of my marine sized dick. Next to the bed were a couple of old ratty looking chairs and at the end of the room I saw a bathroom with an old-fashioned claw foot tub in it and an old rusted wash basin. I shuddered to think what the toilet looked like. At that point I saw my uniform strewn across the floor. I quickly looked down at myself and saw that I was wearing just my knee length black socks my white briefs, and my hat sitting crookedly on my head. My sausage-sized thick dick was still sticking out of the fly opening of my briefs from when I had pissed earlier. It was semi hard, hanging there freely, beads of piss and cum forming on the tip of it.

"H-holy fuckin' shit!!" I gasped. "I-I've been kidnapped and stripped of my uniform!!"

"Right you are you hot stud marine," I heard that familiar sounding voice saying to me.

I looked up and saw him and his buddy towering over me.

"Y-you!!" I gasped. "The two of you!! Y-you're the two guys that congratulated me when I won the prize for my girl… *Oh shit,* where's Laura??? What have you fuckers done with her???"

Thinking of Laura panic filled me and as I ranted on and on I tried to haul myself to my feet but the bigger of the two guys pressed a hand against my shoulder and pushed me back down to my knees.

"Unless you want another good crack across that pretty head of yours boy you'll keep yourself in check," the big fucker said to me, his hand pressed firmly against my shoulder, squeezing it hard, inflicting a little pain.

"Uhhhrrr…" I seethed through clenched teeth. "Laura!!! Are you here honey???"

"Relax Corporal Sommers, your pretty girlfriend is still right where you left her," the bigger of the two men said to me, running a hand over my buzz cut blond hair.

"Yeah, that pretty little thing of yours probably thinks you're still in that men's room pissing your brains out," the other guy said to me mockingly.

"Bastards, if you two have done her any harm," I began to say and then the bigger of the two guys hauled me roughly to my socked feet by one of my muscular upper arms.

"Uhhhfff…" I sputtered as I was lifted from the floor and to my feet.

My dick swung back and forth in front of me, a big piece of tube steak ready for milking. Beads of my piss trickled onto the floor along with the pre cum that was oozing from my dick slit.

"Come here boy, I want to show you something," the big lug said and holding my arm in a tight grasp brought me over to the window of their hotel room.

When we were standing by the window he let go of my arm and pulled the curtain back. From the look of things we were on the fifth or sixth floor of the hotel, overlooking the Saint Gennaro feast. I gulped hard when I saw Laura standing right where I had left her, still waiting for me to come out of the men's room in the restaurant I had been abducted out of.

"Holy shit," I whispered miserably, standing there in just my briefs, socks, and my hat.

"So close and yet so far eh boy?" the big guy asked me mockingly and squeezed my upper arm.

Looking down at all the people freely enjoying themselves sent a shiver of cold fear through me and my dick grew long and fear hard in front of me. Seeing Laura standing there waiting for me, not knowing the predicament I had gotten myself into made me feel even worse.

"What the fuck do you guys want?" I asked, my eyes still staring straight down at my beautiful Laura.

"Just you boy, a hot and handsome marine to have some fun with," the big fucker said and gave one of my ass cheeks a hard squeeze through my briefs.

I looked at him, gulped hard, said, *"oh shit"*, and turned back to the window.

"Laura!!!" I roared wildly, praying that she would somehow hear me, but knowing in my heart that she would not. *"Laura!!!"*

The big guy quickly slid the curtain over the window and as I stood there shaking and trembling uncontrollably the other guy clubbed me over my head again with the metal pipe. Again my hat softened the blow. I said "ohhhrrr gawd", spun stupidly on my socked feet, and hit the floor in a heap. I saw my hat go flying off my head and unconsciousness claimed me again…

When I came to the second time I found myself lying on the big bed on my stomach with my arms stretched wide across the bed and tied at the wrists with mounds and mounds of rope to the bed board.

"Ohhhrrrr gawd, my poor head," I said sheepishly as I came to, pulling myself to my knees on the bed, stupidly putting my butt in the air. "Holy fuck, what is this???"

I pulled wildly and savagely at the ropes around my wrists, trying desperately to get myself untied.

"Hoooorrr gawd, no, no, not this!!" I ranted madly pulling savagely on the ropes, trying desperately to get myself untied.

"Struggle all you want boy," I heard the bigger of the two men say to me. "But once Otis or I tie a knot it stays tied until we decide to untie it."

At the sound of his voice I looked over at the side of the bed. They were standing there, dressed in nothing but their white sweat socks. Their bodies were extremely muscular and their dicks were long, hard, and pulsing in front of them, oozing droplets of pre cum. The big guy's dick was enormous, fat, long, and pulsing like a thing alive. It was a lot bigger than the other guy's dick that was for sure.

"Oh no, no, not this," I grunted miserably, repeating myself, a look of total agony etched on my face. "Guys please; I'm a United States marine after all…"

"All the more reason to do it to you boy," the man named Otis said to me, reached over and grabbed the back of my white briefs.

He tore my briefs straight down the back, revealing my hairless, very white, very like a bowl of whipped cream butt.

"Oh man, look at that butt of his Cleeve," Otis said in awe.

"Yeah, we're going to have a fuck of a time spanking the shit out of him, after we've fucked him a few times each that is," the man named Cleeve said as he mounted the bed behind me, giving one of my ass cheeks a hard slap. "Get those legs spread boy, now, wide!!"

I looked up at him miserably as his big hands closed on my hips.

"Oh fuck," I whispered, choking back tears of rage of humiliation.

He slapped my butt cheek again, and not having any choice whatsoever I did as he had told me, spreading my legs wide apart on the bed. My socked toes dug miserably into the mattress. Cleeve worked a good amount of saliva up in his mouth and spit it harshly down into my gaping, exposed, pink ass hole. I felt it land in there all warm and slick feeling. Then I felt Cleeve's thumbs prodding my hole one at a time.

"Ohhhrrr fuck, get your damned fingers out of my hole you bastard," I ranted angrily, miserably, and in fear.

"C'mon Otis, get up here on the bed and spit into his marine hole," Cleeve chuckled.

Otis climbed up on the bed beside me, hooked an arm around my mid-section, and when Cleeve pulled his thumb out of my hole, Otis spit a big wad of saliva into my hole next.

"Yeah, that's it Otis, let's get his hole good and moist," Cleeve said and spit again into my hole. "For what we're about to do to him he's going to need it to be super wet."

He spit another big glob of saliva into my hole and rapped me a good hard one across the butt cheeks.

"Ohhhrrrr you low-life sons of bitches!!" I seethed through clenched teeth.

Otis tore the rest of my briefs off me, leaving just a few tatters and the elastic waistband of them on me. My dick hung down between my legs, bobbing back and forth with my tight ball sac dangling big under my exposed hole. The two men laughed heartily as they went on taking turns spitting big globs of soupy saliva into my hole, prodding it with their fingers and thumbs, getting me primed for a real hard fuck session. Every time that bastard Cleeve slapped my butt cheeks I wanted to kill him. Otis held tightly to my mid-section with his bear-like arm, holding me in place on that bed I was tied to. Then, Cleeve held tighter to my hips, took position behind me, and began pressing his dick into my slicked hole.

"Ayyyyrrrr gawd, no, *no!!*" I pleaded. "Not this you damned perverts!!"

Even being all moist and slicked up back there did not lessen the pain as Cleeve pushed the whole length of his king sized dick into my hole.

"Ayyyyyyrrrrr!!!" I screamed loudly, my voice echoing off the walls of the seedy hotel room. "You basta-mmmmmfffff!!!"

It was at that point that Otis slapped the big wad of duct tape that had been lying atop the bed board over my mouth, effectively gagging me.

"RRRRRMMMMFFF!!!" I sputtered wildly behind the gag and bucked like crazy on the bed as Cleeve began thrusting in and out of my poor hole, slamming me hard each time he went back in.

His dick felt enormous inside me, filling my hole, stretching it mercilessly as he fucked me and fucked me.

"FFFFrrrrucker..." I ranted behind the duct tape gag. "Fraggots!!!"

As he fucked me like I was some whore Cleeve slapped my ass cheeks hard, sending stinging pain up my spine, really digging his big fingers into the tender white flesh of them.

"Damn, his butt cheeks feel like a babies bottom Otis," Cleeve said and pounded my ass hard with his dick. "Feels so fucking good in there too let me tell you..."

He slapped my butt cheeks again and slammed my hole hard and furiously over and over with his big dick.

"Oh yeah Cleeve, give it to him good," Otis said, smoothing the wad of duct tape over my mouth, his thick fingers trailing over my lips under there.

Cleeve mounted me, his dick wedged deep into my hole by then, and rocked up and down on top of me. He pumped my hole like crazy; fucking me like mad, pile driving my poor virgin ass hole.

"*Ruckers*!!" I shouted shrilly into the gag and bucked madly on the bed. "RRRRRMMMFFF!!!"

"Oh yeah boy, buck that body for me," Cleeve crooned. "I love to feel you fight!"

I balled my bound hands into fists and tears of anger and rage flowed from my eyes.

"Ohhhrrr fuck, ohhh yeah Otis," Cleeve said breathlessly. "His hole feels like it's eating my damned dick."

"Fuck him good Cleeve," Otis said again.

"Fuck, I'm getting close already Otis my man!!" Cleeve gasped and rapped my butt cheeks a good hard one. "Fuckin' hot and handsome marine is going to make me shoot my damned load!!"

Cleeve slapped my butt cheeks harder and harder as he continued jack hammering my hole. I felt like I was being stretched like crazy back there. *Actually I was.*

"Ohhhrrr yeah now Otis, now!!" Cleeve roared like an animal and shot his giant load into my hole. "Ohhhrrr fuck, yeah!!"

"MMmmmffff..." I moaned as Cleeve landed on top of me and

pumped and pumped his load into my hole.

"Ohhh yeah boy, yeahhh," Cleeve whispered, kissing the back of my neck as he came like crazy.

Cleeve's lips felt warm and clammy on the back of my neck and his kissing me repulsed me. When he was done he slowly slipped his dick out of my hole. He climbed off me and stood on the side of the bed as Otis moved behind me.

"MMMMffff!!!" I roared loudly, raising my head up off the bed and looking behind me in disbelief.

Otis was about to thrust his big throbbing python into my hole next.

"Oh yeah boy, here it comes, ready or not," Otis said and plunged his big damned dick into my cum drenched hole.

"RRRmmmfff!!!" I cried and buried my face in the pillow.

Otis' dick felt as bad as Cleeve's as it hit home and he began fucking me, plowing my hole like a madman in heat. I shook and trembled underneath him and when I looked up I saw that Cleeve was sitting on one of the chairs near the bed, his big smelly sweat socked feet propped on the bed, right near my face.

"Enjoyin' yourself boy?" Cleeve asked me with an evil looking grin on his face, his big feet right by my nose at that point.

"RRRmmmmmffff!!!" I ranted at him as Otis thrust harder and harder into my poor hole.

The smell of Cleeve's rancid sweat sock wafted into my nostrils and without even realizing what I was doing, I pressed my nose against his wiggling socked toes.

"Heh heh, knew you would like that," Cleeve said snidely, pressing his toes hard against my nose as I inhaled his sock aroma. "All you marines are sleazy fuckers."

"Ohhh yeahhh fuckin' hot marine you are boy," Otis crooned, drooling madly on the back of my neck as he pumped my hole more and more, slapping my creamy butt cheeks at the same time. "I'm getting close now, ohhh fuckin' A!!"

"Hey Otis, look at the handsome marine sniffing my damned smelly sock," Cleeve said merrily.

"Oh yeaahhh, fuckin' marine likes your feet huh Cleeve?" Otis panted. "Ohhhrrr man feels so fucking good in this hole of his Cleeve!!"

Cleeve's sock smelled of a mixture of foot sweat and work boot leather. I sniffed it heartily and was surprised to feel myself popping a hard-on as Otis went on fucking me and fucking me. Then, like Cleeve, Otis came in gushes into my poor wounded asshole.

"Ohhhrr yeahhh yeahhh!!!" Otis roared on top of me, squirting what seemed like gobs upon gobs of cream into my hole.

It felt so hot back there as his cum flooded my hole. His dick made squishing sounds as he pumped me as he came and came. All the while I had my nostrils pressed against Cleeve's socked foot, inhaling the scent of it. Finally, when Otis was done his dick slipped slowly out of my hole. He climbed off the bed, took the duct tape off my mouth, and stood next to the chair that Cleeve was sitting on, his big feet still propped on the bed right by my face. I licked my dried lips, looking at the men angrily.

"Enjoying yourself so far boy?" Cleeve asked me mockingly and wiggled his socked toes against my cheek.

"You fucking faggots!!" I roared crazily at them. "I swear to God, I will kill you two for this!!!"

"You're going to have to get yourself untied first boy, and like I told you already, when Otis and I tie a guy up he stays tied till we decide otherwise," Cleeve said and pressed his stinking socked toes harder against my nostrils. "Get that tongue working on my foot boy."

A look of despondency came over my face and I stuck out my tongue, running it over the tips of Cleeve's socked toes.

"Can't believe that shit Cleeve," Otis said in awe. "Fucking hot marine is licking your foot."

"Yeah, so it would seem," Cleeve said, a thoughtful expression on his face.

I squirmed miserably on the bed as I felt their cum sluicing and dripping out of my ass hole onto the sheets. My dick hardened more under me as I sucked at Cleeve's socked toes. As much as I couldn't believe what I was doing there really was something about the guy's big smelly foot. I pulled myself up onto my knees and my hard marine sized dick stuck out big, thick, pulsing, and fear hard. My big plum sized balls dangled low under my fucked ass crack. I dug my socked toes angrily into the mattress.

"Shit, fuckin' kid has a whopper of a dick and balls Cleeve," Otis said in awe. "It sure is going to be fun when we milk the fuck outa him later."

"Why're you doin' this to me???" I suddenly blurted, looking at the two men in anger and total rage. Fuckers kidnap me, strip me, fuck me like I'm some cheap whore and now you plan to milk me like a damned cow!! What's the fuckin' point of all this???"

They looked at each other and laughed heartily at my ridiculous question. It was more than obvious why they were doing this to me. I was a young, hunky marine, just the type of jarhead that guys like Cleeve and Otis love to work over. Although most guys would not have the nerve or balls to get the drop on a roughneck marine like me. Cleeve and Otis were the definite exceptions though, and they were living out most guys' perverted fantasies by having abducted me. When they stopped laughing Cleeve pulled his feet away from my face and stood up beside Otis.

"Stay up on those knees boy," Cleeve said with an air of real authority in his voice. "I'm going to lube you for the second round."

"Oh gawd, please, no more," I pleaded, looking at the monster-sized hard-on Cleeve was sporting.

He chortled meanly, reached down, and dealt me a hard rap across my creamy white ass cheeks. I was shaking and trembling as Otis proceeded to pull my ass cheeks further apart. Cleeve reached under the bed, produced a bottle of scotch, and poured some of it into my gaping and exposed hole.

"Ohhhrrr you fuckers," I swore as my head suddenly started spinning.

In what seemed like the next second Cleeve was on top of me and fucking my hole a second damned time. His dick felt just as bad as it had the first time he had fucked the tar out of me. He plowed my poor hole at what seemed like eighty miles an hour, slapping and slapping my ass cheeks hard at the same time. He held the bottle of scotch in his other hand, taking long swigs from it as he went on and on fucking me.

"Ohhhrrr shit!!!" I said through clenched teeth.

Otis sat on the chair with another bottle of scotch in his hand his big feet propped on the bed by my face, and his dick long and hard between his legs. No doubt he was also ready to fuck me a second time. I pressed my nose and mouth against one of Otis' sweat socked big feet. It didn't smell as bad as Cleeve's had, but it sent a chill through me all the same.

"Ohhh yeahhh fuckin' hot marine," Cleeve murmured and plowed my hole deeper and deeper.

"Ohhhrrr gawd and all I wanted was to have a good time at the feast with my girl!!!" I seethed wildly.

When Cleeve came the second time he again filled my hole with his creamy juices, rapping my ass cheeks hard. His dick slipped out of my hole, he climbed off the bed, poured some more of the scotch in my sopping wet ass hole, and then told Otis to take his second turn at me. Otis pulled his feet away from my face and stood up.

"Ohhhrrr you bastards!!!" I cried as Otis mounted the bed.

Cleeve held my ass cheeks apart as Otis poured still more of the scotch into my hole. My head spun wildly and then Otis mounted me and plunged his dick into my hole a second time. I screamed in tortured agony against the pillow as I was fucked again, hard and wildly.

A while later the two men were sitting side by side on the bed, facing away from me, sipping scotch. I was now lying on my back, tied to the bed in a spread eagle position, and blindfolded. The scotch they had poured in my hole had dulled my reflexes so there wasn't all that much I could do as they flipped me over on the bed and tied me to it. Leaning over me with a mean looking grin on his face Cleeve tied a blindfold over my eyes, white cloth, the same kind Laura had tied on me just before we made love the first time.

"You know Otis, we could keep this hot boy of ours here all night *and* all day tomorrow," Cleeve suggested. "I mean, the room is all paid for and all."

"No, you can't keep me here all that time!" I yelled at him. "And I am not your damned boy!!!"

The two men laughed.

"RRRR!!!" I roared and tugged on the damned ropes.

"Corporal Sommers my boy, you are in no position to be telling us what we can or can't do," Cleeve said and I grimaced miserably behind the blindfold. "Now Otis, I have another suggestion…"

I listened in tortured and frustrated agony as Cleeve told Otis that they could call friends of theirs on the phone and invite them up to the hotel room for some real fun with a hot marine.

Fuck, fuck, fuck…" I whispered angrily, in a total rage at that point.

A little while later Cleeve and Otis poured a good amount of the damned scotch over my bound socked feet and knelt at the foot of the bed licking my socked feet, slurping the scotch off my socks.

"Fucking perverts!!" I yelled angrily. "Licking my damned smelly feet, made me lick your damned smelly feet too! *Perverts!!!*"

As they licked and slurped at my feet my dick grew harder between my legs, pointing straight up at the ceiling. Then, I felt the scotch poured over my pink fleshy nipples and Cleeve and Otis were sucking them, hard.

"Mmmm…nice tits boy," Cleeve murmured and bit hard on the nipple that he was working on.

I squirmed miserably on the bed, really ashamed that my dick was hard as a rock and betraying me. When they'd had enough of my nipples Otis took the blindfold off me and I saw that their damn dicks were hard and pulsing again.

"Ready for round three boy?" Cleeve asked me as he and Otis untied my feet. "This time it's *really* going to fucking hurt…"

"Oh gawd," I moaned as Cleeve grabbed my socked ankles and pushed my legs up and over my head, exposing my ass hole.

"Good God, what a position you got me in now you bastard!!" I ranted, my tied hands balled tightly into fists.

Holding me in that twisted position by my ankles Cleeve slowly slid his hard dick into my hole.

"Ohhh yeahhh," Cleeve moaned in ecstasy. 'Warm as a bowl of fresh pudding and tighter than a drum this hole…"

When he plunged in and began thrusting I clenched my teeth as the room started spinning.

"Bastards," I whispered. *"Fucking low life bastards. Shouldn't happen to a marine…"*

Cleeve licked my scotch tasting socks as he fucked me and fucked me, slightly tickling the bottoms of my damned feet. When he came again he filled my hole with his hot jizz. Otis wasted no time whatsoever in scoring a third round of fucking my now aching ass hole. When they were both done fucking me the third time I lay stretched out again on the bed in a spread eagle position as Otis held my head up by the back of my neck, pouring scotch down my throat. What I didn't swallow dripped out of the sides of my mouth and dripped over my chin and onto my chest. Cleeve was squatting at the foot of the bed, licking and slurping at one of my stinking socked feet. Even though my feet weren't tied at that moment I didn't pull my foot away from Cleeve's mouth, because in all fucking honesty it felt too fucking good as the bastard sucked my socked toes.

"Feeling good boy?" Otis asked me as he fed me the scotch, his big hand behind my neck.

"Bastards," I whispered.

"Hey Otis, I just got another fucking great idea!" Cleeve said gleefully, one of his hands wrapped around my foot. "Let's get this kid off the bed."

Otis placed the scotch on the night table, looked down at Cleeve, and reached over to give him a high five. A few moments later I was completely untied from the bed and I was standing between the two men as they held me tightly by my arms in a firm grasp. I struggled in a somewhat drunken stupor as they moved me over to the big table that I would eventually be tied up atop of when they milked and milked the fuck out of my poor dick.

"Fucking bastards!!" I roared through clenched teeth. "Fuckin' let go of me and then we'll see just how tough and mighty you boys are!!! *I'll fuckin' teach you two to fuck a marine's ass!!*"

They moved me next to the table, bent me over it, and pulled my arms out to the sides, really stretching the fuck out of them.

"Owwwwwrrrr!!!" I roared miserably, tottering stupidly on my socked feet, pulling myself up and down on my toes, really struggling in their grasps.

The two men looked at each other, smiled meanly, and yanked me forward real hard. My forehead hit the top of the table, stunning me.

"Uhhhnnnffff..." I sputtered and then felt my wrists being tied to the legs of the table.

When my head cleared I found that my arms were stretched miserably out at my sides and my wrists were roped off to the tops of the legs of the table. My legs were also pulled apart and my socked ankles were roped off to the table legs also. I was standing on the side of that table in a really fucked up and spread out position. My head ached and I would soon have a third lump on it. Not to mention that I was feeling just a wee bit tipsy from the scotch they had poured into me from both ends. My dick was fear hard and pointing straight up under the table as my balls dangled under my ass crack.

"Uhhhrrr, what a fucked up position you two got me in no.... mffffffffff!!!" I said and Otis cut off my words as he pressed the duct tape back over my mouth.

"You're going to need to be gagged for what we're about to do to you next boy," Otis said, pressing the duct tape hard over my lips.

I looked at him in utter agony. When I saw that the two men were each holding a round leather paddle I did not need three guesses to know what I was in for now. On the table in front of me I noticed their leather belts, a big old hairbrush, and two wooden paddles with holes drilled in them.

"MMMmmmffff..." I sputtered and my eyes rolled in my head, a look of utter disbelief on my face.

"Okay Otis, let's spank this boy hard enough to have him hop out of his socks," Cleeve said, stepping next to me and rapping me a good hard one across one of my creamy white ass cheeks with his leather paddle.

"RRRRRRmmmmfff!!!" I sputtered wildly, looking at him in a total rage.

As I looked at Cleeve Otis took his turn and rapped my other ass cheek, just as hard as Cleeve had.

"RRRRmmmmfff!!!" I sputtered again, this time more in pain than in rage.

Then, they were taking turns rapping my ass cheeks mercilessly with those damned leather paddles, harder and harder with each stinging blow.

"UUUUUmmmfffff!!!" I panted behind the gag, sweat breaking out all over me as the two men paddled me harder and harder. "RRRRRRMMMMFFF..."

I scrunched my eyes halfway shut, and stood there squirming and moving my hips back and forth. Cleeve and Otis rapped my ass cheeks more and more, the sounds of it echoing through the dingy hotel room. I curled my toes back under my black socks and my head lolled on my shoulders, sweat pouring from my forehead. I felt the welts beginning to form on my poor butt cheeks, but the men were relentless, they paddled me and paddled me. Shit, they paddled me till I thought I would surely lose my mind.

"*Fruckkkkers...*" I seethed incoherently behind the gag.

Now let me tell you, five to eight raps with a leather paddle is enough to send stinging pain through a guy. Ten to fifteen raps is enough to have that guy screaming in uncontrolled pain and rage, but at that point I had suffered better than thirty raps with those damned leather paddles. And that was just the beginning. The two men went on rapping my ass cheeks harder and harder. Big tears formed in my eyes, and try as I may have I could not stop them from sliding down my cheeks.

"GGGGGRRRmmmffff..." I ranted wildly and almost mindlessly.

They paddled me and paddled me.

"RRRRRHhhhmmmmfff..." I moaned, looking from side to side at my two captors, silently begging them to stop torturing me.

I stupidly pulled myself to my socked toes and the two men paddled the dangling flesh of my sexy ass cheeks. After what seemed like more than eighty to ninety hard raps my ass cheeks felt like they were on fire. They stopped paddling me with the leather paddles. I stood there shaking and trembling in the bondage, sweat rolling off my muscular marine body, and crying, crying in utter and unwarranted pain.

"Damn, look at that Otis, red as a fire engine and hot as a stove," Cleeve said, placing his leather paddle on the table and running a hand over my much wounded ass cheeks.

"Yeah, bet his daddy never spanked him so hard," Otis chortled meanly and I looked at him in total rage.

"And that was just the fucking spanking warm-up," Cleeve said and jammed two fingers deep into my hole.

"RRRRMmmmffff!!!" I sputtered and nearly did jump out of my socks at that point.

I watched in tortured agony as they picked up their belts from the table. They stepped a few feet away from me and began swinging the belts, connecting meanly and hard with my wounded ass cheeks. Each time the tips of those belts connected with my ass cheeks I screamed in agony behind the gag.

"Stay up on those toes boy," Cleeve said sternly as I was about to lower myself to my feet.

I miserably did as he said. When the tips of those belts hit my dangling plum sized balls I literally saw stars and screamed in a high crescendo. The room spun and when they rapped my balls again I nearly passed out from the pain.

"Goddamn Otis, that's fucking awful, rapping a marine's balls with our belts," Cleeve said mockingly. "Let's be careful of that now, Corporal Sommers here may want to be a father some day."

As they laughed and laughed, rapping my butt cheeks harder and harder with their belts I turned my head, looked at them in tortured agony, and sputtered madly behind the gag. Saliva dripped out of the sides of my gagged mouth and sweat poured from my forehead into my eyes. I shook and squirmed in my socks as the two men spent another good ten to fifteen minutes whipping my ass with those damn belts. My hole was stretched wide open and stinging as well.

"Ohhhrr man Otis, working this guy over this way is making me hornier than a fucking toad," Cleeve said and rapped my ass cheeks hard with his belt. "Are you thinking what I'm thinking?"

"Fuck yeah Cleeve, oh fuck yeah..." Otis said anxiously and agreeably.

They gave my ass a few more hard lashes with the belts and I did not need three guesses to know what was coming next. They tossed their belts onto the table and Cleeve went first again for the fourth round of fucking the captured marine. He stepped up behind me, reached around me, grabbed my nipples in his big fingers, and slid his monster-sized dick deep into my gaping hole.

"RRRRRmmmmmffff..." I sputtered angrily at the indignity of it all.

Cleeve squeezed, pinched, twisted, and tweaked the fuck out of my poor nipples as he fucked me and fucked me like crazy. He ran his hands over my hairless and muscular chest, squeezing my pecs like crazy, slapping them hard, and grabbing my nipples again.

"MMMMffff..." I wailed.

"Oh yeah boy, feels as good as before in there," Cleeve said. "Bet this ass of yours is feeling good all around, inside and out huh? Ohhhrrr man, getting close boy, going to fill your hole up with my spunk all over again."

When Cleeve came he rammed hard into me, squeezing my nipples with all he had, really torturing the fuck out of them let me tell you.

"Ohhhrrr yeahhh, yeah!!!" Cleeve grunted as I felt his hot juices flooding my hole.

I stupidly leaned back and laid my head against his shoulder. With his dick still wedged deeply in my hole he leaned down and pressed his lips against my gagged mouth. I closed my eyes in revulsion. When Cleeve's dick slipped from my hole my hole was feeling pretty awful, not to mention how badly my nipples were hurting at that point. My ass cheeks were still on fire and my dick was semi hard between my legs under the table. I was still up on my toes as Otis took position behind me next. Wasting no time he slammed his hard dick into my hole for his fourth fuck at my poor hole.

"GGGGRrrrrnnnfff, *frucker...*" I bellowed.

Otis reached around me, his dick deep in my hole, and picked up the big brush from the table. As he fucked me and fucked me, thrusting like crazy inside me he rubbed the bristles of the brush hard over my sore and swollen nipples.

"Ohhhrrr yeah, sure does feel good in there Cleeve," Otis moaned and rubbed my nipples hard with the brush, really rubbing them raw.

He slapped my pecs with the brush bristles, brushed them all red also, and then rubbed my nipples some more, all the while thrusting in and out of my hole like a madman.

"RRRRRmmmmfff..." I wailed, tears flowing freely down my cheeks now.

When Otis shot his load a little while later he also again filled my hole with his spunk, panting like crazy and rapping me hard on the butt cheeks with that damned brush. When his dick slipped out of my hole I laid my head on the table and sobbed and sobbed. Rage, humiliation, and helplessness all engulfed me at once. Laura's beautiful face passed before my tear filled eyes.

"Ohhh man, best catch we've had in a while eh Cleeve?" Otis asked his buddy.

"Sure as shit Otis," Cleeve said agreeably. "So fucking glad that we're going to keep this kid here overnight and all day tomorrow."

At those words my tears flowed more heavily....

A few minutes or so later they had me slumped half on and half off the damned table. My arms were crossed up behind my back and roped tight at three spots. My legs were pressed together and roped at the thighs, knees, and ankles. My socked feet dangled off the end of the table and I wiggled my toes under my socks in frustration. I was still gagged and the two men were standing at my sides, facing away from me, their big arms wrapped around my mid section, holding me firmly in place. In their hands were the wooden paddles with the holes drilled into them. Misery coursed through me as I realized I was in for still more paddling. Chuckling, the two men began taking turns rapping my ass cheeks hard with the wooden paddles.

"RRRRMmmmmfff..." I sputtered, thinking, "Here we go again!!"

"Oh man Cleeve, this poor kid's butt cheeks are sure taking a beating today," Otis said snidely and rapped me a good hard one across my butt.

"Sure as shit Otis, sure as fucking shit," Cleeve said agreeably. "He'll be a whole new marine when we give him back to that pretty girlfriend of his, tomorrow night."

"After we're done with him he may not want to go back to her," Otis said and rapped my butt cheeks harder and harder with his wooden paddle. He'll be begging his marine buddies to work him over on a daily fucking basis."

The two men laughed insanely and went on and on paddling my poor butt cheeks. Stinging burning pain seared through me. My butt cheeks were welted and twitching by then. I cried big tears and that was when I noticed the glory hole that was cut into the tabletop. I quickly wondered what the hole was for and then more stinging pain as the two fuckers went on and on paddling me with the damned wooden paddles. They were sort of like the paddles that a college active would use on fraternity pledges. And believe me, at that moment I felt like some poor slob of a fraternity pledge. By the time the two men finally stopped paddling me I was amazed at the fact that I had not passed out from the pain. They hauled me to my bound feet and I stood there at attention as the two men each slurped one of my sore nipples into their greedy mouths.

"Mmmmmfffff..." I gasped as they feasted heartily on me.

My nipples swelled up to the size of two cherries on my big hairless chest as the two men ate them with gusto. My dick stuck out long and fear hard between my tied legs. When they stopped Cleeve hoisted me up into his big arms like a bridegroom lifting his bride before carrying her over the threshold of their honeymoon suite. Strong fucker he had to be too because I weigh in at over one hundred and eighty pounds of full marine muscle and he had hoisted me up off that floor like I weighed next to nothing.

"Okay Otis, let's get this marine hog-tied on the table and start milking the fuck out of his dick," Cleeve said and held me over the table.

I looked angrily into his eyes and he dropped me hard atop the table…

"RRRRmmmfff…" I moaned as their hands moved over me to get me into position…

Otis tied the length of rope around the base of my balls before they turned me onto my stomach. Cleeve guided my hard pulsing dick through the hole cut into the table along with my big plum sized balls. As Otis pulled my socked feet back and Cleeve moved my arms to meet my feet I realized what that hole in the table was for. Now I knew what Cleeve had meant when he said that they were going to milk the fuck out of my dick.

"RRRRmmmfff…" I sputtered madly.

So, now you know how I came to be hog-tied atop a table in a seedy hotel room, trapped by two men named Cleeve and Otis. As I lay there listening to them gloat over my damned predicament my hard sausage-sized dick swung back and forth beneath me, twitching, aching to shoot the pent-up load that was stored in my big balls. Little did I know at that moment just how many marine-sized loads the two bastards would force from me, I was going to be milked till I nearly went crazy.

"Okay boy, you ready to start spewing some GI slime for us?" Cleeve asked me and pulled the duct tape off my mouth.

"Arrrhhh shit!!" I grunted as the tape was pulled painfully from my dried lips.

I quickly licked my lips and looked up at the two men with utter rage burning in my eyes.

"Fuckers, this is a fucked up thing to do to a United States marine!!" I ranted at them. "You boys should be showing me some proper respect, but instead what do you do? Bash me over the head, fuckin' kidnap me, strip me of my uniform, fuck the tar out of my hole, and spank me like

I had been a bad boy or somethin'. I swear to God, you two *will* pay for this shit!!"

The two men chuckled meanly and Cleeve gestured at Otis. Smiling, Otis scurried under the table and then I felt his mouth engulf my hard pulsing dick.

"Ohhhrrr gawd, now, *now*" I panted. "Now you fuckers're suckin' my damned marine-sized dick… Ohhhrrr gawd never had a guy suck my damned dick before!!"

"Really boy?" Cleeve asked me, and gave my socked toes a squeeze. "Then you sure have been missin' out on a treat that is for sure. When you get back to your base you should get some of your buddies to suck that hot cock of yours. Bet they would all enjoy milking the fuck out of you a few times each."

"Ohhhrrr yeahhh…" I gasped as Otis sucked me harder and harder.

I had to admit, it felt great as the big fucking guy sucked my dick, slurping his tongue all over it and poking his tongue into my slit.

"Arrrrhhh man, fuckin' marine snatchin' bastard is driving me crazy," I gasped.

"And as we've told you boy, this is just the beginning," Cleeve said, sneering at me as I felt myself getting close to shooting my damned load.

"Ohhhrrr gawd, I'm getting close already you bastards!!" I grunted and spewed a marine sized mess of creamy spunk into Otis' mouth. "Ohhhrrr yeahhh…"

I bucked on that table as Otis sucked and sucked my dick, forcing every drop of cum from me.

"Ohhhrrr shit," I ranted.

When I was done Otis let my dick slip out of his mouth. As I lay there catching my breath Cleeve slipped under the table and slurped my semi had dick into his mouth. He instantly started sucking me, hard.

"Ohhhrrr God, no, no," I panted. "Not again so soon you fucker! My damned dick is all slimy and sensitive after shooting that damned big load."

What a fucked up position I was in, with no way to pull my poor dick away from the two cum hungry fuckers. I felt Otis' tongue moving over my balls and my dick grew hard in Cleeve's mouth.

"Arrrhhh shit, get off my balls you bastard," I grunted huskily. "Fucking going to make me shoot my load again!!"

Then, for the second time I shot a marine-sized load of jizz, right into Cleeve's mouth this time. His tongue swirled over and over my dick in his mouth as ropes of cum erupted from my slit.

"Ayyyyyrrrrr gawd, I'm so sorry Laura..." I squeaked in a high pitched tone of voice.

Goose bumps broke out all over my sweat-covered body and my dick slipped from Cleeve's mouth. He teased the tip of it sadistically with his lips and tongue, sucking just at the slimy tip of it as Otis went on applying pressure to my balls with his tongue. When he slurped one of my balls into his mouth I thought for sure that I would fly off that table. As Cleeve tortured my dick-tip Otis had one of my balls in his mouth. He pulled on it with his mouth, really applying pressure to it at that point.

"Ayyyyyyy," I screeched. "My fuckin' nut man, take it easy with my damned nut..."

Cleeve slurped his lips around the shaft of my dick and began sucking me a third fucking time. My head spun wildly and I tried desperately to get myself untied.

"Gawd, got to get you cum hungry fuckers off my poor dick and balls," I moaned miserably.

But that was a thought, not a possibility. The way those fuckers had me hog-tied to that table I was going nowhere anytime soon. I sputtered saliva on the table in front of me as they sucked my dick, licked and slurped my balls, and forced me slowly toward gusher number three.

"Gawd, never been sucked so much..." I gasped as saliva dripped from my mouth onto the table.

I shot a third load, this time with one of the men's hands holding my dick tightly by the shaft. As he stroked me hard I shot jets of my marine sperm onto the floor under the table. By the time I was done spewing that load I could barely catch my damned breath. I felt their lips rubbing over both sides of my poor aching dick. As they kissed each other around my dick I shook and trembled uncontrollably in the bondage atop the table. When I felt my dick slurped again into one of their mouths I thought I would lose my mind for sure. My dick was numb at that point and my poor balls felt like they were swollen to the size of tennis balls. After a while when I came I suffered what is known as dry orgasms. That can really send a fucking guy over the edge, let me tell you.

"*Ayyyyyrrrrrr gawd, shitty ass way to treat a United States marine corporal...*" I squeaked through clenched teeth as I came for the umpteenth time.

I don't know how many times I was forced to orgasm while hog-tied atop that table. When they'd had their fill of milking me like a damned cow I found myself stretched out on my back on the table, completely untied for the moment. I looked up at my two captors through blurred vision. My dick lay shriveled up and numb between my legs, hanging over my swollen testicles.

"Feelin' good boy?" Cleeve asked me and gave one of my nipples a hard squeeze.

"Y-you miserable perverts," I whispered and lifted my head up off the table.

All the fight had been beaten and literally sucked out of me at that point. I could not lift more than just my head off that damned table.

"Fuckin' beautiful marine we snagged this time huh Otis my man?" Cleeve asked his buddy, running the palm of a hand over my crew-cut head.

"As you would say Cleeve, sure as shit," Otis replied gleefully.

"And tomorrow is going to be another really fun filled day for him," Cleeve added. "By the time he gets back to that pretty girlfriend of his she won't even recognize him."

"*P-please, no more...*" I groaned in a whisper.

Cleeve put a big hand over my forehead and lifted my head higher by the temples.

"Time to go to the land of nod boy," Cleeve said and tightened his grip on my temples.

"Ohhh no, no, please don't," I gasped and Cleeve slammed my head down hard on the table. "UUUUhhhfffff..."

I was stunned for a second, heard Otis ask Cleeve if they shouldn't tie me to the table for the night, heard Cleeve respond that there was no need, adding that I wasn't going anywhere, and then fitful sleep claimed me.

I slowly came to the next morning still lying on my back on the table. I was feeling slightly hung over; what with the fact that they had scotched me up I wasn't all that surprised. My socked feet were dangling off the sides of the table and so were my arms. I stunk of sweat, my asshole was feeling rather lousy, my ass cheeks were still stinging, and my head was aching from all the blows it had been dealt. There was cum smeared on the table that had more than likely dripped from my hole during the night, the way they had fucked me so many times I was surprised there wasn't a major sized puddle there. My dick was soft and shriveled, lying in my tuft of blond pubic hair. Poor guy the way they had milked him so many times last night I wondered if he would ever get hard again. My balls were still swollen from the abuse that had been heaped on them as well. My nipples and pecs were all red and sore after having been manhandled and brushed raw with that damned hairbrush. The need to piss was pretty strong and as I looked around the room through still blurred vision I wondered if I could make it to the bathroom. I wasn't tied down after all. I sat up on my elbows, stupidly leaving my legs dangling off the sides of the table, exposing my much wounded, very fucked, still very moist asshole. As I waited for my vision to clear I thought miserably again of just how awful what had happened to me really was. It should never happen to anybody, let alone a marine of my caliber. I again swore revenge on the two men that had abducted me. Suddenly, through my blurred vision I saw Cleeve come barreling at me, seeming from out of nowhere. He was naked as the day he was born, his monster-sized dick jutting out long and hard in front of him.

"*Ohhh no, no,*" I muttered.

Cleeve grabbed me by my thighs, pulled me forward on the table, hoisted my legs back and over my head, and rammed his big dick into my gaping hole.

"Ahhhrrrr gawds, fuckin' my hole first thing in the mornin' eh you bastard?" I asked miserably.

I gripped the sides of the table as Cleeve thrust meanly and hard into my poor hole.

"Ohhhrrr yeah, good morning to you hot boy!" Cleeve grunted and held me tightly by my socked ankles as he fucked me and fucked me and fucked me.

With the position I was bent into and the way I was feeling all groggy and fucked up there wasn't all that much I could do to stop him. Even being untied for the moment I was powerless against the big guy as he went on and on fucking the tar out of my hole.

"Ohhh man, nothing like that first fuck of the day," Cleeve moaned and slurped his tongue over the bottom of one of my socked and by now stinking feet.

"Arrrrhhh you bastard, shitty thing to do to a marine let me tell you," I moaned softly as the guy pile drove my hole.

As he fucked me I trickle pissed into my nest of pubic hair. I couldn't hold it back and humiliation consumed me.

"Ohhh yeahh, getting there now you hot marine," Cleeve grunted savagely. "Goin' to feed your hole its breakfast…"

Then, Cleeve shot a hot and heavy load of spunk into my deflowered, aching, and stretched hole.

"Ohhhrrr yeahhh yeahhh, feels so good first thing in the morning," he grunted, holding tightly to my ankles as he thrust in and out of me as he came and came and came.

When he was done his dick slipped out of my hole, he let go of my ankles, and I lay there with my feet again dangling off the sides of the table. I squeezed my eyes shut and gripped the sides of the table hard.

"*Bastards,*" I whispered as I felt Cleeve's load leaking from my hole. "*I will kill you and your friend for this…*"

Then, I heard a door close, looked to my side, and saw Otis just coming out of the bathroom. I watched through blurred vision as he approached the table I was on, his big dick jutting out in front of him, wanting its turn in my hole too.

"Ohhh no, not you too you bastard," I groaned.

Before I realized what the fuck was happening Otis had me hoisted off the table, pressed hard against himself with his big arms pinning me to his body, and his dick up my ass. He carried me around the room, bouncing me up and down on his dick as he rammed in and out of me over and over.

"Ayyyyrrrrr…" I screeched. "Got me fucking impaled on your damn fuck stick you bastard!!"

"Whooo, feels so good to have a hot marine like you first thing in the morning boy!" Otis chortled.

"*P-put me down you fucker*!!" I demanded.

Otis held me tightly pinned to him till he shot a morning load of spunk just as big as Cleeve's into my hole, grunting and groaning like a madman as he came and came. When he was done his dick slipped from my hole and he dropped me to the floor in a heap making me land on my ass.

"OOOfff…" I said. "Fuckers,"

I lay there on the musty smelling carpet as the two men towered over me. I saw that Cleeve had a good amount of rope in his hand and Otis was holding a half-full quart sized bottle of scotch. Fuck, I was about to be roped up again and fed scotch as breakfast, and there wasn't jack shit I could do about it. A few moments later with my hands roped in front of me at the wrists I sat on the floor on my wounded ass as Otis held the bottle of scotch firmly wedged in my mouth.

"Yeah, that's it boy, drink it down," Otis said snidely as he poured the contents of the bottle down my throat. "A stud marine like you needs a good hearty breakfast first thing in the morning."

As Otis force-fed me the scotch Cleeve was on his haunches in front of me, his hands on my ankles, squeezing them, looking at me hungrily.

"Goddamn it Otis, he is the most beautiful thing I've seen in a long fucking time," Cleeve said, pulling my more than day old smelly socks off my feet. "When he's done guzzling that scotch let's take him in the bathroom and give him a good shower."

The two men looked across me at each other and laughed meanly. I wondered what I was in for in the bathroom. The scotch burned my throat as Otis forced it down my gullet. By the time I was done drinking the scotch my head was spinning like crazy. Even a big marine like me can't drink on an empty stomach. The two men hauled me to my feet by my upper arms, my bound hands useless in front of me.

"Feeling good boy?" Cleeve asked me mockingly.

"B-bastards…" I whispered and belched loudly.

"Damn boy, you sound really fucked up," Cleeve snickered. "Come on Otis, let's take this kid in the bathroom and give his asshole a good cleaning out."

They hoisted me off the floor by my upper arms and carried me totally naked toward the bathroom.

"Fuckin' bastards!!" I suddenly roared, still in a drunken stupor though. "Untie me and let go of me and then we'll see just how tough you perverts are!! I'll fuckin' teach you to kidnap and work over a United

States marine!!"

In the bathroom they hoisted me into the tub, tied the slack of the rope around my wrists to the shower- head, and I stood there up on my toes as Otis attached a hose to the water faucet.

"Ohhh fuck, no, no, no…" I groaned miserably.

Moments later the two men were taking turns washing out my much abused asshole. Otis held my ass cheeks apart as Cleeve squirted cold water into my hole and then Cleeve would hold my ass cheeks apart so Otis could squirt the cold water into my hole.

"Arrrrhhh!!! You fucking bastards!!!" I roared with my back to them.

The two men laughed hysterically as my body quivered and broke out in goose bumps as they washed out my hole with the cold water. They slapped my butt cheeks, prodded my hole with their fingers, (two and three at a time) and went on squirting the icy cold water into my hole. Twice during the ordeal I pissed but the two men didn't notice.

"Man, he has one of the best asses I have ever seen, or fucked," Otis commented mockingly.

When they were done and when they were satisfied that my ass hole was clean as a whistle they walked me out of the bathroom, my bound hands held rigidly in front of me. My dick was semi hard and dangling between my legs. I was too beat to shit, drunk, and hungry to try anything as they hoisted me onto the bed, stretched me out on my back and roped my bound wrists up to the bed board. Otis sat next to me on the bed, a fresh bottle of scotch in hand.

"You slimy bastards," I seethed just before Otis pressed the bottle to my trembling lips.

As Otis fed me the scotch again my head spun and Cleeve was stroking my sore dick.

"Jerking the kid off eh Cleeve?" Otis asked him.

"Yeah, with what he's been through and with what he's about to go through he deserves it," Cleeve said, slowly stroking me to a major sized hard on.

"Damn, with the way we milked that cock of his yesterday I wouldn't think he'd get hard for days," Otis said, watching as Cleeve stroked me fast, slow, and fast again.

"He's a young tough marine," Cleeve said. "I have no doubt that we could milk him all day and he'll still get hard over and over and over again."

I sipped the scotch down and it burned my gullet. I shot a small spurt of cum a few minutes later, moaning and groaning around the tip of the scotch bottle. When I was done Otis put the bottle down on a night table. I was smashed to put it bluntly. The two men gave my balls a few hard pulls, twists, and squeezes. Otis ran his fingers through the cum that had landed on my chest and fed it to me. I had no choice but to lick my damned cum off his fingers.

"Some of our buddies should be here real soon," Cleeve said as he shoved one of my black socks from the day before into my mouth, gagging me. "And boy oh boy are they in for a real fucking treat..."

"RRRmmmmmffff!!!" I sputtered in my drunken stupor, thrashing wildly on the bed.

Indignity of indignities, having been kidnapped, raped, tortured, and now to have one of my smelly day old socks crammed in my mouth while waiting for a band of perverts to arrive and have their way with me was just too unthinkable. But alas, there was nothing I could do about it, seeing the position I was in after all. And sure enough, about ten minutes later there was a knock on the hotel room door. I silently prayed that it was either the police or my marine buddies come to rescue me. Otis opened the door and six guys came into the room, all of them big burly looking fuckers. At the sight of me they oooed and ahhhed like crazy.

"Whoa!!! Fuckin' hot marine you nailed guys," one of them said.

"Let me at that guy," another of them said gleefully.

"What a sweet lookin' thing he is," still another one of them said.

"Hey Cleeve, here are the bagels and coffee you asked me to pick up for you and Otis," one of the guys said, handing Cleeve a big brown paper bag.

Great, I thought miserably, they get a marine's ass, bagels, and coffee for breakfast while I get scotch. I watched in tortured agony as all the men quickly stripped naked. Damn, from the sizes of their dicks my ass was about to be plowed more than a farm field. The first guy who was naked jumped on the bed, grabbed my ankles, pushed my legs up over my head to expose my hole, and plunged his giant boner into my hole.

"RRRRmmmmmfff..." I roared miserably.

"Good thing you gagged him again Cleeve," Otis said with a grin on his face.

"Yeah, good thing," Cleeve agreed.

While the first guy was fucking me two of the other guys were licking my feet while the rest of them were all reaching for my marine-sized chest, taking turns squeezing my nipples and pecs.

"Fruckers…" I sputtered into my smelly sock gag.

The first guy came in gushes into my hole and then another guy took his place.

"Ohhh yeahhh, goin' to fuck you good and hard you hot marine," the next guy said as he held my ankles aloft, bending my legs back, and plunging his big rod into me. "OOOooo yeahhh…"

It went on like that for what seemed like hours upon hours. My poor hole really took a beating let me tell you. A few of the guys took second and third turns fucking my poor hole and even Cleeve and Otis took another turn each at it, after having consumed three bagels and a large coffee each.

"Damn, by the time we're all done his hole is goin' to be mince meat," one of the bastards said.

Then, when they couldn't fuck me anymore they started feasting on me like vampires. They were all over me like white on rice, licking, sucking, biting, and squeezing my nipples, licking my feet and balls, and even stroking my dick. They forced me to cum two times, making me piss all over myself in between my jizz shots. They delighted in making me drink still more of the scotch and I writhed miserably on that bed as they sucked my toes, bit my nipples some more, and even stole sucks on my sore and aching dick. By the time they were all done with me I was a sweaty stinking mess of a marine. My poor, poor hole was stretched beyond reason and cum oozed and dripped from it like crazy. It was true my hole had been turned into a sloppy and slimy cunt.

"Ohhh man, that was fucking great," one of the guys said as he got dressed.

"Yeah, never fucked no marine three damn times before," another of the men said as he pulled his shirt on.

"RRRRRmmmfff!!!" I sputtered wildly at them.

"Heh heh, hey boy, how's that sock of yours tasting?" another of the guys said and leaned down to jiggle one of my toes.

I looked at him through blurred vision, a look of death on my face.

"Hey Cleeve, when are you and Otis going to let this kid go?" the first guy who had fucked me asked.

"Not till this evening," Cleeve said. "He has a pretty little girlfriend we have to give him back to. Why do you ask?"

"I was thinking I would come up for lunch," the guy said and all the men laughed meanly and sadistically.

By the time the six guys left the room it was early afternoon and Cleeve and Otis decided to feed me lunch. With my hands now roped tightly behind me and the long black sock that had been used to gag me tied over my eyes as a blindfold I sat on my knees, sucking Cleeve's damed dick.

"RRRRmmmfff..." I sputtered miserably around the big tube steak that Cleeve had wedged in my mouth.

He pumped his shit tasting dick in and out of my mouth, feeding it to me, prepared to make me eat the globs of cum that he would shoot at any moment. His big hands moved over my sweat soaked buzz-cut blond hair. I had never sucked cock before, and this was beyond humiliating.

"Oh man Cleeve, that is awful, jamming your cock in the kid's mouth after it's been up that sweet ass of his," Otis said snidely.

"Yeah, sure as shit Otis," Cleeve grunted, pumping in and out my mouth like crazy. "And it's goin' to be up his sweet ass a few more times before this is all over. Fucking kid makes me so damned horny I can fuck him all day. Ohhhrrr yeahhh, getting there now Otis!!"

Then, Cleeve grabbed my earlobes, jammed his dick further into my mouth, and shot his big wad.

"Ohhhrrr yeah, yeah, that's it boy, swallow my load!!" Cleeve grunted madly as he thrust far in my mouth. "Lunch is served..."

His cum tasted all soupy and salty as it filled my mouth. I gulped it down, not really having much of a choice after all.

"MMMMFffff..." I gasped.

When Cleeve was done his dick slipped out of my mouth. Before I could even say a word Otis' big fat throbbing tool was in my mouth next.

"Oh yeah kid, that's it, suck my dick," Otis said, feeding me his pulsing and shit tasting dick.

They each fed me two loads of cum. When they were done I was kneeling there with my head hanging down in utter torment. My hands were still tied and my sock, turned blindfold was still tied over my eyes. I stupidly wondered where my other sock was. I licked my cum caked lips and tears of rage and humiliation burned behind my eyes...

"Damn, I am beat," Otis said. "Fucking kid drives me wild."

"Yeah, while we're waiting for our next wind let's use some of our equipment on him," Cleeve said and the two men laughed insanely.

I grimaced behind the blindfold, wondering what the equipment was that they were talking about...

If Cleeve and Otis were anything, they were resourceful, that was for fucking sure. Like two boy-scouts they had come prepared, with plenty of what they called equipment. I choose to call the equipment instruments of torture. Cleeve pulled me to my feet by my arms and took the blindfold off me, leaving it hanging around my neck.

"Kid, you are in for it now," he said and hoisted me off the floor.

"You bastards!!" I roared as Cleeve set me down atop the table again on my back. "This is sick and fucked up what you're doing to me!!"

Gawd, it wasn't bad enough that they had kidnapped me, fucked the shit out of me numerous times, tortured me, and made me suck cock. Now they were going to use a host of mean and torturous devices on me. Otis knelt atop the table over my head, his big dick and balls dangling in my face as Cleeve stood at the foot of it. Otis held my feet aloft and pulled back by my ankles, holding them as far apart as possible, exposing my slimy and cum drenched asshole. My sore dick and swollen balls hung just over the table, hanging there so that Cleeve could snap a tight fitting cock ring around them.

"Ayyyyyrrr shit, what're you plannin' on doin' to me now man?" I groaned miserably, watching Cleeve through the V of my spread legs.

"Damn Otis, this hole of his is really stretched looking," Cleeve said and then worked a leather ball separator onto my poor swollen nuts.

"Ayyyyyy..." I moaned as my balls hung painfully away from each other, the pressure on them and my dick immense at that point. "*Gawd, my poor dick and balls you guys...*"

"Well Cleeve, with the way we and our buddies fucked him more than a few times each it's no wonder that his hole is looking pretty stretched out at this point."

The two men laughed meanly and Cleeve stepped away from the table for a moment.

"You fuckers…mmmmffff…" I snarled and then Otis lowered his big smelly balls onto my mouth.

"Go ahead Kid lick my nuts for me," Otis said snidely. "Clean all the sweat off them."

With no choice other than to do as I was told I pressed my tongue against Otis' balls and began lapping at them.

"Ohhh yeah, that feels real sweet Kid," Otis said breathlessly and licked one of my bare feet.

As I was licking Otis' big balls Cleeve stepped back over to the table. I couldn't see what he was holding in his hand but I soon found out what it was.

"Okay you handsome fucking marine, I sure as shit hope you're ready for this," Cleeve said and stuck two of his big fingers deep into my violated hole.

"GGGrrrmmmmfff…" I sputtered, spitting saliva all over Otis' balls.

He lowered himself on me some more, giving me a mouthful of his nut sac at that point.

"Damn kid, this hole of yours is still moist enough that I won't even have to waste time lubing you up again," Cleeve said, jiggling his fingers around in my hole. "Not to mention that I won't have to start off small either."

Then, I saw what Cleeve had in his other hand as he held it up. I gulped hard around Otis' balls as Cleeve held up a fat, long, mean looking dildo shaped vibrator. He pulled his fingers out of my hole and lowered the dildo.

"RRRmmmmfff…" I wailed maniacally, silently begging the big bastard not to shove that thing inside me.

Holding one of my aching and swollen balls in his fingers Cleeve lifted my dick and balls away from my exposed asshole. Actually, I think he just wanted an excuse to squeeze the fuck out of one of my poor tortured balls. Then, he slid the monster-sized dildo shaped vibrator slowly into my hole, thrusting in and out a little with each push he gave it.

"RRRRmmmmfff…" I wailed around Otis' balls in my mouth.

I squeezed my eyes shut as Cleeve pushed the damned thing

further inside me. Then, he turned the dial on the bottom of it and it came to whirring life in my hole.

"GGGGGRrrrrmmmmfffhhh…" I screeched.

It felt as if a thousand little pinpricks were assaulting the walls of my hole all at once. When Cleeve pushed the thing still further into me he turned the dial a second time. It felt worse, hot, and goose bumps sprang up all over me. My head spun away.

"Oh yeah Otis, poor hunky marine is suffering now," Cleeve said meanly. "Keep feeding him your balls."

"Yeah, you said it Cleeve, feels great," Otis moaned.

Then, Cleeve pushed the vibrating dildo all the way inside me and turned the dial to the last notch. The thing felt like it was whirring at one hundred miles an hour inside me. It felt as if it were literally eating the walls of my hole. Cleeve thrust it in and out of me slowly and then fast and then slowly again. I was sweating and stinking by then and my dick (amazingly enough) grew hard between my legs.

"RRRRRRFFFFF!!!" I sputtered madly, fearing that I would go completely out of my mind at that point.

Otis sucked my toes as I continued lapping his better than cleaned up balls at that point. My legs were numb and feeling awful, having been held up and spread for so long. Cleeve fucked me and fucked me like crazy with that vibrating dildo, sending waves of electric heat through my hole. My dick lay hard and sore against my stomach area a good amount of pre cum oozing from my slit.

"Ha!!! Look at that shit Otis, fucking marine is hard as a fucking rock!" Cleeve chortled. "Looks like he's learning to like this after all."

"See if you can get him off Cleeve," Otis said anxiously. "After he shoots a load that thing jammed in his hole will really fucking drive him crazy!!"

"Yeah, a few good pulls should do it too," Cleeve said and grabbed my hard on.

I panted like mad as he stroked me fast, fucking me and fucking me and fucking me with that dildo.

"RRRmmmmfff!!!" I wailed as I shot a somewhat good-sized load onto my chest.

But then, agony and utter torment and pain as after I shot my load my hole became super sensitive. It felt a hundred times worse now as Cleeve fucked me with that damned thing. And not to mention that because of the cock ring and ball separator snapped on me my dick stayed super hard and pulsing.

"MMMMFFF…" I muttered and tears slid from the sides of my eyes.

"Oh yeah Kid, lick my balls…" I heard Otis say as my head swam away some more.

A short while later Cleeve slid the vibrating dildo out of my hole and Otis pulled his balls out of my mouth. He lowered my legs on the table and climbed off it. I lay there panting and sweating, crying with the pain I was in. The cock ring and ball separator was still on my dick and balls and my hands were still securely tied behind me. Gawd!!!

"B-bastards," I whimpered miserably. "When the fuck're you two going to let me go already???"

Laughing, the two men looked at me, looked at each other, and kissed each other on the lips….

The next devices that Cleeve and Otis used on me nearly brought an end to my poor balls, which were already in unspeakable agony. And speaking of unspeakable, before being tortured I found out what had become of my missing sock. Off the table and leaning against a wall with my hands tied behind me Cleeve crammed one of my rancid black socks into my mouth and tied the other one over it, effectively gagging me. I got to say it because it's true; gagging a guy with his used smelly socks is a downright shitty thing to do to him. It really sucks. Standing at my other side the mindless Otis was holding my upper arm in a tight grasp and teasing one of my nipples with the fingers of his other hand at the same time.

"RRRMMMFF…" I sputtered madly, looking at Otis in a rage.

"Bet you're feeling really wasted and used up at this point eh you handsome fuck?" Otis asked me mockingly and pressed his lips against my gagged mouth. "Shit man, and I thought you marines loved being worked over."

"Okay Otis, let's get him started," Cleeve said and held up a pair of sharp teethed tit clamps.

I groaned miserably. Cleeve opened the jaws of the tit clamps and slowly brought them toward my swollen and sore nipples.

"Mmmmmffff…" I moaned, looking at him beseechingly, silently begging him not to clip the damn things onto my poor nips.

With a fiendish look on his face he placed the open tit clamps around the nubs of my nipples. I breathed unevenly in fear as Otis held me in place by my upper arm, squeezing it tight. Then, Cleeve closed the tit clamps right onto the tips of my poor nipples. They hung there and pulled down meanly on my nips.

"*RRRRRMMMMMFFFFF*!!!" I squealed, feeling as if the damn clamps would literally pull my nipples right off my chest.

I slammed my head back against the wall in total defeat and saliva spilled from the sides of my gagged mouth. My dick was still hard with fear and jutting out in front of me, beads of piss forming at the tip of it. The cock ring and ball separator was still on me and the pressure on my dick and balls had become mind numbing by then. Yeah, I was a marine in a real fucked up situation that was for sure. I writhed miserably against that wall as the two men ran their hands over my hairless chest, squeezed my butt cheeks, and tugged on the chain attached to the tit clamps.

"GGGGRRRRRFFF..." I reeled madly as saliva dripped from the sides of my gagged mouth.

"Ha!!! Bet you're feeling real fucked up now huh Kid?" Cleeve asked me, and he and Otis moved me away from the wall. "Okay Kid, you're in for some real fucked up torture now."

A look of agony mixed with rage filled my face as Cleeve produced a pair of metal ball bearings with long strings attached to them. When the two men hunkered down at my dick and balls I didn't need three guesses to know where the ball bearings were going to hang. As the two men looked longingly and hungrily at my dick and balls I miserably shook my head "no" from side to side, desperately trying to get my hands untied. To really put the screws to me the two men each slurped one of my swollen and aching balls into their mouths.

Rmmmmmmffff!!!" I gasped and tottered on my bare feet.

My body arched forward, causing the tit clamps to pull harshly on the tips of my poor nips. When my balls were beyond swollen and pulsing like crazy the two men each tied one of the ball bearings onto them, holding the ball bearing in their hands.

"Okay, on three Otis," Cleeve said, holding his ball bearing between his thumb and first two fingers.

"RRRRmmmmffff!!!" I sputtered wildly, knowing all too well

what was about to happen.

"One, two," Cleeve began as I violently shook my head from side to side. "And three…"

The two men let go of the ball bearings, sending them plunging toward the floor. It seemed to happen in slow motion. The ball bearings plummeted to the floor, stopping just as they were about to hit the floor. My balls were jarred painfully and the pain went searing through me.

"RRRRRmmmmfffffff!!!" I gasped and straightened up real fast, sweating and groaning in unspeakable pain.

Cleeve and Otis quickly sprang to their feet at my sides.

"Okay Kid, at attention, *now!!!*" Cleeve barked at me.

I looked at him and if I could have would have spit in his face. He gave me a hard slap on the ass and I snapped to attention, standing there in utter pain.

"Now he looks real miserable," Cleeve said and tugged on the chain on the tit clamps as Otis squeezed my butt cheeks, kissing the side of my neck at the same time.

When the pain became beyond intense I passed out cold, falling into Cleeve's arms….

I came to a while later, in the early evening to be exact. I found myself in the alley behind the restaurant I had been abducted out of. I was slumped on the ground against a brick wall, wearing just the tatters of my underpants. The tit clamps, ball separator, and cock ring were off me. My hands were untied too. My uniform, socks, and shoes were on the ground next to me. My first thought was that I could not believe that the two fuckers had left me totally naked in an alley. My second thought hit me like a brick falling on my head. I looked down and to my horror saw that there were two homeless men squatting at my sides, sucking and slurping my damned swollen to the size of cherries nipples.

"Ohhh shit, what is this???" I blurted in fear and total confusion. "H-how'd I get down here?"

I looked down again and watched a few seconds in anger as the two homeless guys really feasted heartily on my poor nipples. With their mangy tongues they licked my nips real hard, flicking those tongues over the hard tips of them. Chills spiraled up my spine as their horrid looking tongues licked and licked my poor nips. With their lips and tongues they slurped the fuck out of them. With their front teeth they bit them mercilessly and tugged on them till I thought they would literally bite the fucking things off my chest.

"G-get off my nips you guys!" I ranted, about to pull myself to my feet.

I pressed my palms against the ground to give myself leverage to get up, but then, the homeless man with the scruffy beard grabbed the dildo that Cleeve and Otis had left wedged in my hole. He began thrusting the dildo in and out of my marine hole, fucking me like crazy as he and his buddy went on and on eating my nips with utter gusto.

"Ayyyyyrrr gawd, fucking bastards that kidnapped me will pay for this!" I ranted and grabbed my hard dick.

As the two homeless guys slurped, sucked, and ate my nipples and screwed my hole with the dildo I stroked my big dick, my balls aching at the same time. After a while I let loose a torrent of white juicy marine spunk.

"Ohhhrrr gawds, fuckers, eating the fuck out of my damned nips!!" I ranted madly.

When I was done shooting my load the two homeless guys got to their feet and walked slowly out of the alley.

"Oh man, just love eating a good pair of tits every once in a while," one of the homeless guys said. "Even if it is a guy's tits, I mean shit, that kid's tits tasted better than a woman's."

"Yeah, if we see those two guys that dumped that kid back there we have to thank them for it," the second homeless guy said.

I sat there for a few minutes, my hand over my face, sobbing like a baby. When I was finally able to pull myself to my bare feet I was holding my ass cheeks tightly together around the dildo *still* wedged in there. I pressed the palms of my hands against the brick wall and with that damned dildo held firmly between my cheeks I pissed a long yellow stream of marine piss. I was still sobbing as I pissed and pissed and pissed…

When I emerged from the alley a little while later I was wearing my uniform minus my underpants. I had thrown the dildo in one of the garbage pails in the alley. Walking slowly I saw that the streets were already crowding up with people enjoying the Saint Gennaro feast. Through somewhat hazy vision I looked toward the spot where I had left Laura waiting for me the night before. To my astonishment she was just then approaching the spot, a look of anguish on her beautiful face. I quickly dashed over toward her. At the sight of me her eyes lit up and we ran toward each other. She threw herself into my arms and held me tighter than ever before.

"Oh God, Mark!!" Laura cried, her arms around my upper neck, clinging madly to me. "Mark, what, what happened to you? I waited for a half hour before I went into that restaurant looking for you."

"I-I'm okay Laura," I whispered, my eyes scrunched closed, fighting back tears.

"When I went to the police they told me I had to wait at least twenty four hours before filing a missing person's report," she said shakily and kissed my earlobe. "Mark, where were you? What happened to you?"

"I-I don't," I began, my arms tightly around her too. "L-Laura, I'm really hungry. Can we maybe get something to eat?"

She pulled away from me and looked at me through tear filled eyes. I was choking back my own tears, not wanting her to see me cry. Actually, I didn't want Laura to know any of what had happened to me.

"Of course Mark," she replied.

We walked together into the Italian restaurant I had been abducted out of and sat down at a vacant table.

"You look awful," Laura said, holding my hand atop the table. "What happened to you?"

"I-I don't remember Laura," I said softly. "I remember going into the bathroom, I recall getting dizzy, and then I think I remember just wandering around."

"Are you sure?" she asked me. "Mark, I thought someone had kidnapped you or something."

"Heh heh, why would someone want to kidnap me?" I asked her and tightened my grip on her hand, trying real hard to be cool about it all. "God Laura, I love you…"

"I love you too Mark," she said.

At that moment the waiter came over to us to take our order. I ordered two appetizers for myself a bowl of soup, and a main course with a side order of pasta. I was more than famished. I was out rightly ravenous.

After we were done eating Laura and I went out to enjoy the feast for a while before returning to our hotel room. As we walked the streets of the feast I kept a sharp lookout for Cleeve and Otis. No way was I going to let those two bastards off, not after what they did to me.

When Laura and I returned to our hotel room I made sure to get undressed by myself in the bathroom, lest she see that I was not wearing underpants. I emerged from the bathroom after a long and very much-needed shower. I was wearing a fresh pair of white underpants to cover my welted ass cheeks and a white tee shirt to cover my mangled nipples. Laura didn't protest when I told her that I really wanted to go to sleep... I was sure that she knew there was something I was not telling her, but she didn't ask. She never pursued it...

I am still with Laura, I have not seen Cleeve and Otis since that fateful night, but someday, someday I will see them again. And when I do I will make sure they pay dearly for what they did to me. Shitty thing to do to a United States marine, let me tell you...

Justin Adams' Story

"Ohhh God, you fucker!!!" I grunted miserably and in utter pain as the guy held me practically impaled on his pulsing and monster-sized cock facing away from him. "*Fucking me another time you bastard!!*"

"Oh yeah guy, and this is just the beginning," he said breathlessly, his lips right by my ear. "My buddy Otis and I can go on and on fucking this sweet ass of yours all night long!! By the time we're done with this hole of yours it'll be mincemeat. Shit, you're going to have a sloppy fucking cunt back here when we get finished with you. Looks like that pretty wife of yours over there is going to have to find herself a new husband."

He slurped on my earlobe and held me tightly against himself as he thrust in and out of my hole like a madman for the second time that night. His big muscular arms were wrapped around me and he was rubbing my smooth hairless chest, his fingers tweaking and torturing the fuck out of my nipples every few seconds or so. His arms wrapped around me felt like two steel vises as he held me pinned against him. My hands were roped tightly behind me as he fucked me and fucked me, in my own bedroom, with my wife nearby and watching the whole humiliating spectacle. As I was fucked harder and harder by the big hulking guy named Cleeve his mindless buddy Otis hunkered down in front of me. I nearly jumped through the ceiling as I watched him slurp my semi hard cock into his mouth.

"Ohhh fuuuuuuccccckkk man, *th-this shit is total insanity!!*" I garbled angrily and miserably.

"Oh yeah, that's it Otis, suck this guy's cock, suck him real fucking good!" Cleeve chuckled meanly. "We'll see just how many loads he can cook up for us!!"

I looked helplessly across the room at my wife. She simply sat there stone faced, in total shock perhaps, watching in more than horror as her husband was savagely worked over and raped. Streams of tears cascaded from her beautiful eyes and a look of total helplessness was etched on her face.

"Oh yeah guy, maybe next time you'll tear the subscription tape with your name and address on it off the magazine after you're done reading it," Cleeve snickered and again slurped meanly on my earlobe, thrusting his big cock deep inside me.

"Ohhh God!!!" I grunted, my head thrown back as he slid me up and down on his throbbing hardness.

As I was fucked and sucked I thought more than miserably about what he had just said and recalled how a Sports Oriented magazine had gotten my wife and me into this jam…

"Ohhh!!!" I seethed and my mind wandered back in time to the morning before…

It was a Wednesday morning like any other. The alarm clock went off at 4:00 AM, I pushed the button down on it, silencing it, and climbed out of bed. I padded in the dark on my bare feet to the bathroom to shower, leaving my wife sleeping soundly. She works at an office job and doesn't have to get up till 6:15 AM. I work for a mail shipping company and have to be up and at the job by 6:30 AM. Wearing just my white boxer shorts I stood in the bathroom brushing my teeth, staring at my sleepy eyed reflection in the mirror. Getting up extra early in the morning before my shift starts affords me some time for my breakfast and the newspaper in a diner nearby where the mail shipping office is that I work at. When I was done brushing my teeth I used the toilet and then climbed into the shower, the warm water cascading over my thin but wiry body. I let the warm water soak me before soaping myself up starting at the shoulders. Like any other morning I dressed for work in my company uniform (black pants and a pullover purple shirt with the company logo on it) and black high-top sneakers. I dressed as quietly as possible in the bedroom with the lamp light from the living room slightly lighting the room for me.

"Mmmmmm, Justin?" my wife murmured at me in a half doze.

"Yeah Babe?" I asked her as I sat on the edge of the bed tying one of my sneakers.

"Is it time for you to go to work already?" she asked me. "Seems like we just went to bed last night."

"I know, I feel the same way Babe," I said and leaned over and kissed her cheek. "Love you Babe."

"I love you too Justin, so much," she whispered and fell back to sleep.

Smiling, I stood up, took my wallet off my night table, put it in my pocket, and walked out of the bedroom, closing the door quietly behind me. In the kitchen I pulled my denim jacket on, grabbed my keys from atop the refrigerator along with the sports oriented magazine I had received in the mail the day before, and left the apartment. I walked the few blocks from our apartment to the 50th street train station. I waited the usual five minutes or so for the five fifteen B train to arrive, standing on the platform reading the latest issue of the sports magazine. A famous football player had retired from his longtime career and the Mets had lost miserably recently. These were the two top stories in the latest issue. When the train arrived in the station I boarded as usual, sat in the usual vacant seat, and settled back for the ride that usually took anywhere from forty-five minutes to an hour. As I sat there reading the article about the football player's retirement I suddenly felt as if I were being stared at. Being a New Yorker makes one sensitive to things like that. I glanced up and noticed two big guys sitting across from me. I had never seen them on the train before. When you take the train at the same time every morning you get used to seeing the same faces practically everyday. You don't say anything to those same people that you see everyday; you just get used to seeing them on a regular basis. I figured the two burly looking guys were new in the area or just returning from visiting with someone overnight. They were both dressed like construction workers, mustard colored work boots, worn looking blue jeans, and flannel shirts. I could tell that they were both very muscular, no doubt from the work that they did. The bigger of the two guys had dark short-cropped hair and very intense looking dark brown eyes. The other guy was somewhat shorter and on the stocky side. He had light brown wavy hair and light eyes. When the bigger of the two guys saw me notice them staring at me he pursed his lips and smiled at me. I could not believe it; most people in New York would simply have looked away, whereas this guy smiled at me. Ignoring them, like most New Yorkers would, I returned my attention to my magazine and stretched my legs out in front of me, pressing the bottoms of my sneakers against the pole in the center of the train-car. A few stops later I glanced up again and saw that the two rugged looking men had stopped staring at me. The train-car was filled with the usual crowd of blue-collar workers, a few suits, and some female office workers. While the train was riding over the Manhattan Bridge I again felt eyes staring at me. I glanced up and sure enough the shorter of the two construction worker type guys was looking at me. His eyes seemed to be drinking me in, devouring me actually. Now I never had anything against gay people, live and let live you know. I felt slightly uncomfortable though and simply ignored him, trying to keep my attention focused on the magazine I was reading. Even if they were faggots there was no way I was going to mess with them, being that they were both the size of brick shit houses. When the train pulled into Grand Street (the first stop in Manhattan) I decided to change my seat. As people disembarked the train I stood up and moved to a seat at the other end of the car, out of view of the two staring men. Alas, that would be my first mistake. I would make the second mistake when I disembarked the train about ten minutes or so later. At 6:15 AM the train pulled into the 50th Street station in Manhattan, Rockefeller Center to be exact. I stood up and rolled up my magazine, done with it at that point. As I got off the train I didn't see that the two-construction worker type guys got off the train as well, at the other end of the car. I mindlessly and with no thought about it whatsoever dropped my magazine in a trash can on the platform. I sprinted up the steps and out of the station. The two construction worker types waited till the platform was just about deserted before extracting my magazine from the trash can I had just chucked it into. They weren't interested in reading about sports, no, not these two, that was for sure. What they were interested in was the subscription tape affixed to the bottom of the cover of my magazine. The tape with my name, address, borough, and apartment number imprinted on it. The two men smiled with sick satisfaction…

The workday was pretty much like any other. I battled traffic delivering and picking up mail packages from various companies throughout Manhattan. Actually, delivering and dropping off packages was how I had met my beautiful wife two years ago. I had been delivering a package to the office building on Fiftieth Street, which is right near the office my company is situated in. When I walked off the elevator on the tenth floor I walked straight into the reception area. Seated behind the receptionist's desk was the most beautiful blond girl I had ever seen in my life.

"May I help you?" she asked me, looking up from the computer she was pecking away at.

God, she was more than beautiful, even her voice when she spoke to me seemed to flow over me like velvet.

"Uh yes," I began, trying to sound as professional as possible. "I have a package here for a Mr. Stone."

I put the medium-sized box on the desk along with a pen and a clipboard.

"I'll sign for it," she said, looking at the sender's address. "Oh good, Mr. Stone has been expecting this."

She picked up my pen and scrolled L. Richards on the line with her boss's name at the other side of it. I looked at her signature and smiled at her.

"What does the L stand for?" I asked her politely.

"Linda," she replied and took the small package.

"Ah, Linda, did you know that in Spanish Linda means beautiful?" I asked her.

"Really?" she asked me, her lips pursing and forming the most beautiful smile I had ever seen.

"Yes, it does," I said. "I'm uh, I'm Justin."

"What does Justin mean in Spanish?" she asked me with a grin on her face.

"I have no idea," I replied with a wide smile and we both laughed.

"Well, I better get this package to Mr. Stone," she said, getting to her feet.

She was wearing a white blouse with a short beige skirt. My God, I think I loved her on sight. I guessed her age to be in the early twenties, somewhere around the same age as I. I also took in the fact that she was wearing neither a wedding band nor an engagement ring.

"Uh Linda, if you're not busy after work this Friday, do you suppose I could talk you into maybe having some dinner with me?" I boldly asked her, wondering if I had just put my foot in my mouth.

I mean, lets face it, just because she wasn't wearing a wedding or engagement ring didn't mean she didn't have a boyfriend.

"No, actually I'm not doing anything at all," she replied, standing there holding her boss's package that I had delivered in her beautiful slender fingered hands.

My heart thundered in my chest so fiercely that I thought for sure that she was able to hear it. Holding her boss's package she was standing there smiling at me, seeming to be trying to etch my face into her memory.

"Well great," I said happily. "Do you like Chinese food? I know a really good place on Forty-Fourth Street and Broadway, unless you prefer something else."

"Chinese food would be fine," she said. "Meet me here say about five thirty?"

"Sure, five thirty would be great," I said ecstatically. "Just great."

Within a year and a half we were married and living in the Boro Park area of Brooklyn. I was the happiest guy on the planet...

The workday that day went by pretty quickly for me. On lunch hour I stopped at Linda's job to see if she wasn't too busy to have lunch with me. It was a beautiful day and I figured we could eat on the promenade at Rockefeller Center. We bought sandwiches and sodas and sat in the sun eating lunch. I had forgotten all about the two guys on the train who had been checking me out that morning. Not that I would have told my wife about them anyway, that wasn't something a guy wants his wife knowing, that a couple of mean looking dudes were checking him out lustfully. But those two guys had not forgotten me bud. I didn't see those two guys from the train sitting nearby as I sat there having lunch with my wife. If I had seen them I would also have seen that my discarded sports oriented magazine was crammed in the back pocket of the bigger of the two guy's jeans...

"Do you think you'll have to work late tonight?" I asked Linda.

"I don't think so," she replied. "Why do you ask?"

"Oh, I don't know, I thought maybe we could stay up late and read," I said in a silly sounding tone of voice.

"Ah, is that all?" she asked me with a grin and we leaned in close to each other and kissed gently on the lips.

This time I did not feel it as the two men stared at me as I was kissing my beautiful wife. By the time Linda and I were finished eating the two men were gone. They didn't need to follow me all day. They had my name and address after all…

I called it quits at five PM on the dot that day. I parked my mail company van in the underground garage, signed out for the day, and headed home on the subway. That night would prove to be the most fateful night of my life…

Linda and I had a light dinner and went to bed early that night. We made love like crazy before finally going to sleep. God almighty, we loved each other so much. The day when I met Linda she admitted that when she saw me walk into the reception area of the building she worked in she thought that I was the cutest guy she had ever seen. It was as if we were meant for each other from the very beginning. But on that night things would change. Things would change more than drastically. What I didn't know was that the two men were parked across the street from our apartment building in their van. When Linda reached over to turn off her night-light the room was plunged into darkness save for the light of the moon shining through the thin shade of our open window. It was a warm night but not warm enough for the air conditioner so we had left the window open. Bad mistake, very bad mistake. Linda was wearing a white see-through nightgown and I slept as usual in my white boxer shorts, the tip of my cock peeking through the fly opening. Linda always said that I looked adorable yet erotic in my boxer shorts with my cock peeking out of them. She said it was like I was teasing her. More often than not I would be awakened in the middle of the night by Linda putting her arm around me, reaching over and taking my cock in her hand, reaching into the fly opening of my boxer shorts to get to it. Many times I would wake up with Linda holding my hardness in hand while we had been sleeping. And of course many times when I woke up with my hardness in Linda's hand I knew just where to put it next… As we slept peacefully we did not hear the two men making their way up the fire escape toward our window. Being that we live in a side apartment there was no one on the street to see the two men as they made their ascent to our open window. They silently crept into our apartment through the bedroom window. They drank in the sight of me laying there in just my boxer shorts, my cock tip peeking sexily out of them, my body shining in the moonlit room. The bigger of the two men made his way over to our bed in silence as his buddy closed the bedroom window. It wouldn't do after all to have any people who may be outside to hear what was about to happen in our bedroom. The sound of the window hitting the sill jarred my wife and me from sleep.

"Wh-what was that?" Linda asked her eyes slowly coming open.

"I-I don't know," I began to reply when my sports oriented magazine landed on my chest and the bedroom light was turned on.

"Wh-what the???" I blurted and looked up to see the two guys from the train that had been checking me out standing in our bedroom. *H-holy fucking shit!!!*"

At the sight of the two men in our bedroom Linda screamed in out right horror. I grabbed the magazine off my naked chest, saw that it was mine from the day before, and the horrible truth hit me like a ton of bricks. The guy who had closed the window brought the shade down.

"*Wh-what the fuck do you guys want?*" I asked through trembling lips as I sat up on the bed.

Suddenly, and with lightning like speed the bigger of the two guys standing next to our bed punched me a good hard one in the stomach, dead center, knocking the very wind out of me. I gasped the word "Ooooffff!!!" and sat doubled over in intense pain, gagging and retching. The guy then grabbed me by my throat and with one hand literally hoisted me off the bed.

"ACCCCHHH!!!" I screeched as my bare feet hit the floor.

"J-Justin!!!" Linda screamed reaching for me as the bigger of the two guys hauled me bodily across the room and over to his buddy.

I stumbled stupidly on my bare feet and the other guy caught me by my upper arm. The pain in my stomach from the blow I'd been dealt was still flaring as the second guy held me tight by my upper arm; me standing there just about doubled over. With a wicked looking grin on his face he gave me another good hard punch to the epicenter of the old gut.

"Oooooffffffff!!!" I gasped again, louder this time, thinking for sure that I would spit up blood.

The guy let go of my arm and I landed at his feet in horrific pain. The guy by our bed, as I said the bigger of the two grabbed Linda by her wrist and yanked her toward himself.

"L-let go of me!! Oh my God!!" my wife screamed in terror. "Oh my God, *Justin!!*"

"Leave her alone you bastard!!" I roared and despite the pain I was in tried to get to my feet, but the other guy backhanded me hard across the face, sending me back to the floor, in more pain. "Uuuuuhhhnnnnfffff!!!"

As Linda struggled in the bigger guy's grasp he turned and looked down at me fiendishly. My head was spinning from the blow I had just endured and I could not believe what he said next. I actually thought that I was hearing things.

"It's not your pretty wife that we want Mr. Adams," he said. "I thought you would have realized that on the train this morning."

"On, on the train this morning? J-Justin, what is going on?" Linda screamed in total terror as she tried in vain to pull out of the guy's strong grasp. "*Wh-what is he talking about?*"

He yanked her to her feet on the bed by her wrist and pointed a meaty finger in her face.

"Listen to me bitch and listen well," he said threateningly. "Keep your yap shut and your handsome husband over there may just survive this night!!"

"Wh-what???" Linda asked, tears forming in her fear crazed eyes.

At that moment Linda realized she was not going to be raped. Although, at the same time she wasn't all that thrilled at the fact that her husband *was* about to be raped. I tried again to get to my feet but as I sat up the other fucking guy again backhanded me quickly and painfully across the face, sending me sprawling back to the floor.

"Uhhhnnnnn," I said stupidly as I again hit the floor, tasting blood in my mouth this time.

"We saw that gorgeous stud of a hubby of yours on the train early this morning pretty lady," the big guy said to my wife, practically drooling at the mouth as he spoke, moving her over to a chair that we keep in the bedroom. "And to be perfectly honest we've been talking and thinking about him all fucking day."

"Yeah, talking about all the things we want to do to him," the guy who had backhanded me chortled meanly.

Linda looked over at me in disbelief as the guy sat her in the chair and all I could do at the moment was lye there on the floor in pain.

"Pretty as you are honey we would really rather get to know your hot looking hubby, no offense," the big guy said fiendishly. "Way I see it; he'll put up more of a struggle than you ever could."

"Yeah, and we love a good struggler," the other guy chortled.

"J-Justin, wh-what is he talking about?" Linda asked me again, shaking like a leaf as the big guy ran the tip of his finger under her chin.

Looking at my sports oriented magazine on the floor all I could do was look helplessly over at my wife. My face was throbbing where I had been backhanded, I still tasted blood in my mouth, I could feel my face swelling up and my stomach still ached too. No doubt that my face would be more than swollen come the next day, if I lived to see the next day that is. I didn't know yet exactly what these guys planned on doing with me.

"L-look, take whatever you want," I said from the floor, feeling the spots on my face where the guy had rapped me already starting to swell up. "J-just don't hurt my wife."

I didn't dare try to get up again, for fear of being backhanded a third time…

"Now that's what we want to hear," the guy who had backhanded me twice said from behind me.

Suddenly, he reached down, grabbed my ankles and yanked me up off the floor in an upside down position.

"Arrrrrrrrhhh God, p-put me down you bastard!" I ranted.

"J-Justin!!" Linda bellowed as the bigger guy was roping her to the chair with rope that he'd had in his jeans pocket.

I watched helplessly from the upside down position I was being held in, my arms flailing uselessly out at my sides.

"Do as you're told guy and your pretty wife will be fine," the guy holding me by the ankles said mockingly.

I shuddered as he lowered me, gave one of my big toes a fast slurp and then hoisted me high again. I was actually afraid he was going to drop me right on my head.

"P-perverts!!" I seethed miserably as tingling sensations coursed through me from having had one of my toes sucked on.

The guy hauled me bodily across the room and tossed me onto our bed.

"OOOOFFFFFF!!!" I said stupidly as I landed on the bed.

By the time I got my bearings Linda was tied tightly to the chair, her hands behind her, rope wound over and over her upper body, accenting her cleavage area and her pretty feet tied tightly together.

"No more noise bitch," the bigger guy said to her, pointing his big meaty finger in her face. "Now, sit back, relax and enjoy the show!"

"Fucker, *bastards, you can't talk to my wife like that!!*" I snarled and rejuvenated by a feeling of total anger made to get to my feet and off the bed. "I'll fucking kill both of you for this shit!!"

But when I was halfway up the other guy again grabbed my ankle, yanked it hard and sent me sprawling back on the bed.

"Yuuuuhhhffffff!!!" I sputtered madly.

He then yanked me hard off the bed, banging me bodily against a wall.

"OOOOOOFFFFF!!!" I gasped and fell into a semi stupor.

The guy held me against the wall with one hand pressed up against my throat. With his other hand he punched me another good one right in the epicenter of my stomach.

"HUUUUFFFFFF!!!" I grunted through clenched teeth and slid to the floor as the guy let go of my throat.

From somewhere far away I heard Linda's voice softly crying my name. Then, the two men hauled me up off the floor and threw me back onto the bed. I landed in a heap and looked up at them in a daze, all the wind and fight knocked out of me.

"Man, what a hot looking piece of ass he is Otis," the bigger of the two guys said, looking down at me hungrily.

"He sure as fuck is Cleeve," the other guy said, as I looked up at them in total fear, slowly climbing out of the stupor I had been knocked into. "I'm really glad we decided to ride the train back to Manhattan after our little jaunt with that other dude here in Brooklyn rather than take a service cab. This little New York vacation has proved to be very worthwhile."

They snickered meanly and I fleetingly wondered whom the "other "dude" in Brooklyn was that they were talking about.

"Fuckers, y-you got my address from the subscription slip on my damned magazine?" I seethed.

"Sure did handsome guy," the guy named Cleeve said and reached down to rip my boxer shorts off me.

He grabbed them roughly by the fly slit, hefted them forward till my legs were pulled up off the bed for a moment and then tore them easily from my body.

"Shit!!!" I seethed more than angrily as my boxers' came off me and I flopped back down onto the bed. "S-so this is why you two perverts were checking me out huh?"

For calling them perverts Otis gut punched me again good and fucking hard bud…

"HOOOOFFFFFF!!!" I gasped in total surprise, not having expected it that time.

He gut punched me hard enough that I thought I was going to fall right through the mattress.

Then, I lay there completely naked and in awful pain as the two men took in the sight of me…

"Man oh fucking man, his skin looks as soft as velvet Otis," Cleeve said, pulling more rope from his jeans pocket. "Let's get this dude roped up and start working him over!"

"R-rope me up?" I asked through clenched teeth. "No, no fucking way you bastard!!"

As I made again to get up off the bed and try to subdue the big guy first the other guy, the one named Otis gave me a good hard rap across the back of my head. I again fell to the bed, my poor head spinning, Linda softly crying as she watched the awful spectacle. Cleeve reached down, grabbed one of my wrists and in a fast move had me flipped over onto my stomach.

"Knew it, I fucking knew it, a nice round melon shaped butt," Cleeve said as Otis yanked my hands behind me and roped them tightly at the wrists.

I was more than shaking in fear and choking back tears, tears for my poor wife and what she was about to witness and tears for me for what I knew I was about to endure. Cleeve gave my melon shaped (as he had so aptly called them) ass cheeks a few hard squeezes and slaps each, the sounds of the slaps resounding in the bedroom. A few moments later I was standing with my legs spread wide as Otis squatted behind me, holding my ass cheeks slightly apart and slurping, licking and drooling in my ass hole. My eyes spun in my head as the strange sensations of what was being done to me coursed through my being. Cleeve knelt in front of me sucking my cock and tongue bathing my balls while his buddy ate my hole...

"Ohhh God almighty, sleazy perverts," I grunted and looked over at my wife in total despair.

She was looking at me in what seemed to be a combination of shock and total disbelief. I mean, how many wives get to see their husband having his asshole eaten by some guy while another guy sucks his cock and tongues his balls? God, Linda and I had just made love less than two hours ago. I wondered despondently how I had come to be in this more than fucked up position...

Cleeve sucked one of my balls into his mouth and applied awful pressure to it with the tip of his tongue.

"Arrrrrrhhh Shit!!!" I ranted miserably.

"Oh Justin, your poor balls," Linda said stupidly and woefully from across the room.

My wife knew that my balls were super-duper sensitive. When we had first started having sex I told her that my sensitive nuts were off limits. But now there wasn't all that much that I could do to stop the big hulking guy from torturing the fuck out of my poor balls, as Linda had so aptly called them. As Otis flicked his big mangy tongue around in my hole, chills sped up my spine and all over my body. He drooled some more into my hole and literally sucked the walls of it.

"EEEEeeeerrrrrrrrr Gods, feels like this fucking guy is goin' to eat my hole right off my ass," I seethed.

Otis then spread my ass cheeks wider yet and plunged his tongue deeper still into my most private crevice.

"Ohhh ssshhhiiiiitttt," I garbled, looking across at Linda through slightly blurred vision as Otis' tongue burrowed deeper and deeper inside me, drooling in my hole like a madman, sucking up his saliva.

Fuck, it sure felt awful these two helping themselves to my most intimate parts. Cleeve then let my now hard cock slip slowly out of his mouth. I was breathless at that point. The bigger of the two guys stood up in front of me and tweaked my small pink nipples a few times, twisted them, yanked them and pinched them hard.

"YARRRRRRhhh, *damn it man, leave my fuckin' tits alone,*" I yelled at him.

Smiling fiendishly he pulled up hard on my poor nipples, forcing me to my tiptoes.

"Ayyyyyyyyrrrr shit!!!" I ranted as Cleeve held me up on my toes by my poor nipples.

"My buddy is not eating your hole to get you feeling good handsome guy," Cleeve said, moving his face dangerously close to mine. "He's moistening you up back there, getting you primed for a real hard heavy-duty *fuck session.*"

My jaw dropped down in shock at the sound of those words and I choked back tears of revulsion as Cleeve squeezed and yanked up my nipples even more.

"Ohhhr!!!" I blurted.

"You should be thanking him for getting your shit chute all good and soaked up back there let me tell you," Cleeve went on, moving his mouth toward mine as I shuddered. "*Because we are going to fuck that sweet ass of yours like you won't believe!*"

That said Cleeve clamped his mouth down on mine, hard...

At that moment I was glad he was holding me up, even if it was by my now very sore nipples, seeing as what he had just said had my head more than orbiting...

Again I heard Linda's voice from far, far away calling out my name as Cleeve kissed and kissed me...

As he did so I felt as if I was being given the kiss of death. Otis eating my hole sent more and more chills through me. His tongue flicked around and around in my now sopped hole like crazy, his saliva dripping in there and seeping from the bottom of my crevice and down the backs of my thighs. I wondered how much further the guy would try and stretch my ass cheeks apart, seeing as it felt like he had them at the ripping point. Cleeve kissed me a few seconds more and I was shocked to realize that I had been sliding my own tongue around and around in his big mouth. My cock was hard as a rock and pulsing in front of me, sticking out of my small patch of pubic curly hair. God almighty, what was up with that shit anyway? I'm straight as a damned arrow and these guys feasting on me had gotten me rock fucking hard.

"Okay Cleeve, he's wet as an overused sponge back here," Otis then said to his buddy, taking his mouth off my asshole, letting go of my ass cheeks. "I think our handsome guy here is ready."

Cleeve let go of my nipples and grinned maniacally down at me...

"Ohhh no, no, you blasted bastards," I ranted as they hoisted me off the floor and back over to the bed.

It was Cleeve who went first. He shucked his jeans down around his ankles along with his white under shorts. He sat on the side of our bed and I was then looking at one of the biggest fattest and most sinister looking cocks I had ever seen in all my life. Not that I had seen all that many cocks mind you, except in porn movies and of course the locker room at the gym. Cleeve's tool was alive and pulsing, twitching with a life all it's own it seemed, pre cum oozing heavily from the muscular guy's wide slit. God almighty, that cock was ready to fuck some poor unsuspecting hole days ago from the look of it. I guessed that the guy would be able to go more than a few times. It caused me to wonder if his mindless buddy Otis was stacked up the same way in this department. Cleeve had obviously waited till he found just the right hole to relieve his pent-up juices. And alas, it would be mine to bring him relief...

"Oh God, oh God, y-you can't be serious about this," I whispered despondently and looked over at Linda with total fear etched on my face.

"Handsome guy, we are more than serious," Cleeve stated sternly.

Linda looked back at me utterly helplessly. Then, in what seemed like a fast motion Otis hoisted me up and began lowering my hole onto Cleeve's big monster-sized cock.

"Ohhhrrrr no, *God no, d-don't do this to me you guys!!*" I ranted miserably. "I-I'm no faggot after all!"

"Neither are we Mr. Adams," Cleeve said mockingly, gripping my ass cheeks and spreading them apart to accommodate his cock as it started sliding painfully into me. "But this sure is entertaining let me tell you."

He slurped at one of my nipples, teasing the tip of it with his tongue as Otis moved me further down onto his pulsing organ. God almighty, it was more than pulsing, I could feel it throbbing as it entered me inch by inch...

"Ohhh you fucker!" I seethed.

"Ohhh yeah, fucking A Otis, better and tighter than any pussy any day," Cleeve said in delight.

Cleeve's big over-sized cock actually felt like a thing alive inside me as he entered me more and more, inch by painful inch, stretching the walls of my hole further and further apart. Holding me by my upper arms Otis moved me up and down on Cleeve's throbbing cock, thrusting me down further each time.

"Ohhh fuuucckkkkk!!!" I groaned, feeling my most private crevice being abnormally stretched.

"Oh God, stop it you monsters! PLEASE STOP IT!!" Linda cried from across the room.

The two men looked over at her meanly and she quickly pursed her lips together.

"One more word from you pretty lady and it'll be you impaled on my big cock!" Cleeve panted, sliding in and out of me like crazy by then.

"No, *no*," I quickly pleaded with him. "Fuck me man, fuck me hard! Just leave her alone! Do whatever you want to me! Just leave my wife out of it!"

"Now that's what the fuck we want to hear handsome guy," Cleeve said, patted me on the cheek and thrust harder still into me.

"Ohhhrrrrr Gods almighty!!!" I ranted breathlessly, in miserable pain.

Otis' saliva dripped from my hole as Cleeve's pre cum moistened me up even more back there. After a little while the only sounds that could be heard in the room was the squishing of Cleeve's giant cock in and out of my hole and our panting, he in ecstasy and me in pain…

"Oh man Otis; I could fuck this handsome guy all night!" Cleeve said and held me tightly by my sides as he and Otis rocked me up and down on his big hard cock. "As a matter of fact I think I will."

The men laughed and chortled hysterically, my wife silently cried and I did my best to endure it all so that they wouldn't decide to use her instead of me.

"Ohhh fuck, I-I'm getting close already you gorgeous fucking guy," Cleeve said in my face and held me tighter and tighter.

"AYYYYYYYYY Gods," I reeled in agony as he jammed me down hard on his cock, forcing every inch of his pulsing fuck stick inside me, holding me there as he began to shoot his load, and I do mean *load*.

"Ohhh yeah, fucking A Otis, the guy has nice tight hole that is for sure!" Cleeve panted and I felt his hot thick juices flooding me deep and long as his hardness pulsed and throbbed deep inside me.

"Ohhh God, fucking bastard, *th-this is a lousy thing to do to a married guy!*" I gasped with my head thrown back, the pain of Cleeve's cock spearing me immense. "Fuck that, this is a lousy thing to do to any guy!"

It seemed to go on and on as Cleeve shot his load into my hole. He held me tightly pinned down on his cock as he shuddered and grunted as he flooded me and flooded me with his juices. When he was done he gave me a few last thrusts and then slid me slowly off his hardness, he and Otis holding me by my arms.

"Ohhh fuuuccckkk, him sliding off my cock is giving me chills Otis!" Cleeve panted madly.

They literally tossed me to the floor and Cleeve leaned back on the bed, his big cock slowly going soft and dripping the last remnants of his cum.

"*Bastards,*" I whispered from the floor, looking over at my wife in total despair.

Cum and saliva dripped embarrassingly from my fucked hole and onto the floor as I tried to pull myself to my feet. I wasn't all that successful though, as Otis picked that moment to lower the zipper on his jeans and bring out his fat (not as big and long as Cleeve's if that was any consolation) hard cock and his big mangy looking balls. He grabbed me from behind and slid his hardness into my cum and saliva soaked hole.

"Ohhhrrrr G-gods, y-you too fucker?" I rasped angrily, as the guy wrapped his big beefy arms around me and literally lifted me up and down off the floor as he thrust in and out and in and out of me.

I looked like I was doing a stupid dance of pain as he bounced me up and down on his gaping hardness, my own hard cock swinging up and down in front of me, my balls swinging temptingly in my sac.

"Looks like this gorgeous guy is really enjoying this eh Otis?" Cleeve asked. "Judging from that hard on he's sporting I think I'm right."

"N-no way you pervert!!" I spat, raging at Cleeve. "*No fucking way!!*"

"Oh yeah, oh fuck, fucking A, beautiful guy you are Justin Adams!!" Otis whispered slovenly and hoisted me up and down on his cock.

"P-put me down you fucker!" I seethed through clenched teeth.

"Oh Justin," I heard Linda cry from across the room.

"Ohhh yeah, fucking A again Cleeve, I-I'm going to shoot my damned load!" Otis announced in breathless and wild passion.

That said the guy bent me over and thrust in and out of my hole as he, like Cleeve seemed to cum in massive torrents inside me. I felt his hot steamy juices flooding my hole as he spanked my ass cheeks, as he seemed to cum and cum and cum…

"Goddamned bastards!" I said warily.

When Otis was done the two men stood me between them and ran their big mangy hands all over my lanky chest area, squeezed my nipples and made sport of squeezing my hard cock, tugging my balls and kneading my butt cheeks.

"Y-you got what you came for," I said miserably as they handled and squeezed me like I was some cheap whore. "Why don't the two of you be on your way now?"

"Be on our way?" Cleeve asked me, sounding as if he were in shock. "*Be on our way?* Mr. Adams, we're just getting started on you."

And so, Cleeve sat on the bed, held me facing away from him and proceeded to jam his newly hard cock into my hole a second time as Otis got busy sucking my cock…

My mind returned to the present and the misery I was suffering at the moment.

"Ohhh yeah, looks to me like we're going to be here all night Otis," Cleeve said, his big hard cock jammed tightly in my hole.

"You said a mouthful Cleeve," Otis responded holding my hard cock momentarily in his hand before slurping my guy greedily back into his mouth.

"Ohhh fuccckkkkk!!!" I grunted breathlessly.

I noticed, or at least thought that I noticed my wife looking hungrily and lustfully over at my cock in Otis' hand before he had resumed sucking it. As I had mentioned Linda loves holding my cock in her hand while we're sleeping. All rational thoughts were cut off at that moment because it was *at that moment* that Cleeve announced that he was ready to shoot his second load. And to my utter disbelief and horror I found myself cooking up a good-sized load for the mindless Otis to chow on.

"Ohhh yeah guy, fucking Justin Adams, goin' to fill your shit chute a second time with my man juices," Cleeve grunted throatily in my ear.

I clenched my teeth because for myself as well there was no holding it back as Otis' practically siphoned my cock in his mouth.

"Ohhh Gods, f-fucking guys, got me creaming like a bitch in heat!" I ranted, my head arched back again.

The pain of Cleeve's cock deep in my hole and Otis sucking me off combined sent me into a lather of mixed and confusing feelings. I was in a state of forced ecstasy, sheer and horrible pain and mental anguish. My wife watched as Otis chowed down heartily on my hefty load of creamy sperm. Cleeve and I shot our loads together, he into my hole and me down Otis' mangy gullet. Otis suckled and sucked me even as I spurted and spurted rope after rope of my good stuff, wanting no doubt to force every damned drop of it from me. Needless to say my mind was a jumble of confusion. After the way Linda and I had made love earlier it was amazing to me that I could cook up a batch of slop that big. Okay, I'm a young and virile guy, but still… And also, never, *never* before had some guy chowed down on my juices. When we were done Otis wasted no time in impaling me on his fat cock for a second go round. All thoughts of my confusion and all other thoughts were instantly cut off as his cock speared me again.

"Ohhh no, no man, don't you fuck me a second time too you bastard!" I ranted madly, my poor hole burning and feeling beyond sore at that point. "Ohhh Gods, th-this feels worse than before!"

"That's because you just popped your nut handsome guy," Otis said meanly, sitting on the bed and rocking me up and down on his hardness, me facing him this time as he looked up at me, stealing licks at my nipples every few seconds. "Right after a guy shoots his load every part of him becomes real sensitive to the touch, mostly his hole and his tits."

"Ayyyyyyyrrrrrrr shhhiiiitttt, yeah, like a straight guy like me should know about that crap!" I grunted miserably and angrily.

As Otis rocked me up and down and up and down on his fat cock for the second time I saw Cleeve squatting down beside my bound wife.

"Looks like that sexy husband of yours is really enjoying all this huh bitch?" he asked her meanly.

She simply looked at him in revulsion and despair.

"I guarantee little lady that your marriage will never be the same after this," Cleeve said and placed a hand on one of her thighs. "What we're doing here will enhance your marriage to that sexy stud of a guy like you won't believe."

"G-get your hands off me," Linda whispered as Cleeve's hand moved across her thigh and toward the center of her legs.

"Oh yes, no denying it bitch, you are enjoying the show," Cleeve said and slid two fingers into my wife's soaking wet pussy. "Either you're wishing it was you we were doing or you're wishing it was you somehow fucking that sexy husband of yours."

Cleeve glanced over at Otis ramming and ramming my hole with his hard cock, listened to me grunting and swearing, sneered for a second and then returned his attention to my wife.

"He sure can take it up the old wazoo wouldn't you say?" Cleeve asked her with a mean looking grin on his face.

"No, *no,*" Linda panted miserably and in ecstasy at the same time. "G-get your hands off me you bastard!"

He slid his fingers deeper inside her and she shook with ecstasy, watching as Otis hoisted me up and down on his fat, fat cock, thrusting in and out and in and out of me. My toes were pressed hard against the floor as the guy did his work and my (again) hard cock was grinding against his flat tight and washboard-like stomach area.

"Ohhh God, Good Gods almighty," I seethed.

"Yeah, look at that bitch, your hubby is hard as a rock all over again," Cleeve said breathlessly and teasingly prodded my wife's pussy hole with his fingers, moving them in still deeper. "Don't you wish he could give it to you now?"

"Oh God, *oh God you miserable rapist!*" Linda panted and stole a glance at Cleeve's dangling meat stick.

"Oh yeah, you like *my* cock eh bitch?" he asked her, his voice deep and throaty now. "Bet you're wishing that I would fuck you good with it eh? Tell you what though; the next time that handsome husband of yours fucks the tar out of this wet and squishy pussy of yours you think of me okay?"

"Fucking bastard!!" Linda ranted at Cleeve as he worked his fingers around and around inside her, driving her practically insane with it.

"Going to cum eh bitch?" Cleeve teased her.

And then, I could not, simply *could not* believe what happened next. Otis shot his second load in my hole, holding me jammed down good and tight against his hardness as he flooded me. I thrust my big hard cock against his (sexy?) stomach and shot my second load as well. And my wife, my wife orgasmed also as Cleeve's fingers did their work inside her.

"Ohhh, oh God, Justin," I heard my wife panting, looking lustfully over at me as I sat rigidly positioned on Otis' cock.

"Ohhh yeah, yeah guy, fucking A!!" Otis panted like an animal in heat as he seemed to cum and cum like crazy inside me.

All rational thoughts were cut off for me again as I shot my load, crying out my wife's name but being worked by the mindless Otis.

"Man oh man, I am feeling all left out here," Cleeve said, slipping his fingers out of my wife's hole and getting to his feet, his cock hard, primed and ready to go as Linda looked up at him blankly. "I know you want it bitch, but your husband needs it a tad more at the moment."

Turning his back on her Cleeve laughed mockingly…

Oh Good God and it would of course be me that the guy had his third go at. When Otis was done sopping up my hole for the second time and I was done shooting my load all over his stomach Cleeve was waiting for me.

"Come here guy," Cleeve said grabbing my arms from behind me as Otis slid me off his cock and quickly impaled me on his monster-sized cock, facing away from him.

"Ohhh no, no, not again you bastard!" I seethed as Cleeve wrapped his arms around me and grabbed my nipples.

"Beautiful fucking guy," Cleeve whispered, slurped my earlobe and thrust deep inside my poor sore hole.

God, I could feel the walls of my hole being stretched even more as the guy fucked and fucked me. It seemed that Cleeve and Otis were both twenty-four hour a day sex machines. Cleeve teased my nipples meanly and twirled his fingers around the nubs, really sending me into a sexy feeling spin. He fucked me harder than hard, slow and meanly. I caught a glimpse of Otis squatting next to my wife and doing to her what Cleeve had done to her just minutes ago.

"N-no, leave her alone!" I panted.

Linda had her head thrown back and seemed to be cumming again and again and again…as she watched me being speared and as Otis fingered and fingered her. Fuck, fuck, *fuck, what was up with that anyway?*

Was seeing her poor husband suffering the way I was getting her all worked up? But fuck it all man, I could not get mad at her, because, because, damn it all, *my cock was hard as a rock again as Cleeve rammed me the third time.*

"Oh yeah guy, you're both going with the flow now,' Cleeve said and let go of my nipples, only to reach down and grab my hardness in one hand as he went on and on fucking the tar out of me. "We'll have you both cumming again real soon, and this time I'll join in the sexy concert."

"Maybe we should send them a bill for this Cleeve," Otis said merrily as he finger fucked my wife.

Linda looked across the room at Cleeve fucking me and her eyes seemed to fill with a primitive looking hunger. Her breath came in short angry gasps.

"Ohhhrrr yeah, getting there now guy," Cleeve announced in breathless abandon. "G-going to fill this sweet shit chute of yours again."

That said Cleeve started stroking my hard and by then sore cock. As he shot his load inside me I shot another load as well, and across the room my wife was moaning in some kind of passion right along with us. The sounds of ecstasy and pain filled the room...

When Cleeve was done he let me slide off his cock, shuddering as I went. I landed unceremoniously on my ass on the floor.

"Feeling good guy?" Cleeve asked me as he packed his cock and balls back into his jeans.

"Y-yeah, feeling real fucking great," I seethed, looking miserably up at him. "J-just what I've always wanted, to be ass fucked by two sadists like you guys."

Otis slid his fingers from my wife's hole, stood up and packed his cock and balls in his jeans as well.

"Please man, like I said before, you got what you came for," I mumbled up from the floor. "Just get the fuck out of here now and leave us alone..."

The two men looked at each other and laughed hysterically...

"Leave you alone guy?" Cleeve asked me laughingly, sounding astonished. "Mr. Adams, all of that was simply the warm-up. Now we're ready for round two..."

I gulped hard as the two men went on laughing and laughing...

A few minutes later I found myself on our bed slumped over my wife's and my pillows, which Otis had tucked under me at the crotch area. My well fucked and cum and saliva sopped ass stuck up like two shining moons. My feet and legs were stretched out as far as possible and tied off at the ankles to the legs of the bed… My semi hard cock was pulled under me and visible… I didn't need three guesses to know what I was in for now…more of the same that I had suffered thus far…

As I lay there like a tied up chicken of sorts Otis was laying on the bed behind me, his legs dangling on the floor, his face buried in my exposed and sore crevice.

"Ohhh fuuuccckkkk," I gasped as Otis' tongue again burrowed around and around in my hole, flicking around in there, his lips sucking at the walls of it.

He licked and ate his and Cleeve's juices out of my hole, seeming to be greedily taking back all that they had pumped into me. My wife was still sitting tied to the chair and Cleeve was squatting next to her, smoking an expensive smelling Cuban cigar.

"Yeah, that's it Otis, while we're waiting to get our second winds we'll tease the guy's hole a while," Cleeve said and puffed heartily at his long thick cigar, blowing the smoke in my wife's face. "And I have just the best way right here to really tease the fuck out of him…"

"*Bastards,*" Linda whimpered. "My poor husband, leave him alone already…"

"Ohhh shiiiiitttt," I rasped as Otis stretched and spanked my ass cheeks, burrowing his tongue deeper still inside me.

When he'd had enough of eating my crevice he got up off the bed and Cleeve stepped over to me next…

What he did was more than mortifying to say the least. His cigar wasn't even halfway smoked. With one hand palming one of my ass cheeks he slowly slid the saliva soaked end of his lit cigar into my sopped hole.

"Hooooooooo, shit, wh-what're you doin' man?" I gasped and lifted my head up off the bed, trying to crane my neck around to see what he was doing, although I knew all to well. "Ohhh God, no, no, get that mangy stogy out of my asshole man!!"

Otis grabbed a handful of my hair and turned my head facing forward…

Cleeve slid the cigar further into my hole. I could almost feel the heat of the lit end of it. I found that the soaked walls of my hole were actually sucking the cigar in… My head seemed to spin away… Cleeve thrust the cigar in and out of my hole a few times, literally fucking me with the damned thing. The smell of the smoke from the thing wafting up from my hole was awful to say the least… God, it was like I was smoking the cigar, but puffing on it with my ass hole rather than my mouth…

Cleeve and Otis squatted at my wife's sides, each of them taking turns finger fucking her, seeing who could get her more breathless.

"Yeah, look at my cigar in your cute hubby's hole bitch," Cleeve said as ashes fell off the cigar in my crevice. "Bet he's wishing it was my cock in there keeping that hole of his nice and warm again. What do you think?"

Linda simply stared blankly at the cigar, as the walls of my hole seemed to be sucking it in and out… What a sight that was let me tell you, me propped up on two pillows, my ass in the air and a lit fat cigar smoldering in my hole…

When the cigar was halfway burnt down Cleeve slid it out of me and puffed it hard…

"Mmmmm, nice raunchy ass taste Mr. Adams," Cleeve said with sick satisfaction.

After forty-five minutes or so had gone by I heard the sound of Cleeve's zipper being pulled down for the second time that night…

"You ready for round two Mr. Adams?" Cleeve asked me as I glanced over at him next to the bed, a new cigar sticking out of his mouth, the old one crushed on our bedroom floor, his cock harder than hard all over again as it hung out of his jeans along with his big plump balls.

"*Oh God, no man, not again, please,*" I pleaded desperately.

With her eyes opened wide in outright horror my wife watched helplessly as Cleeve mounted the bed behind me on his knees, his monster-sized cock aimed right at my gaping hole…

"Ohhh yeah, still nice and warm and real fucking tight," Cleeve grunted around the cigar in his mouth as he again plowed me.

"Ohhhrrrrrr shhhiiiiittt," I gasped and my head popped straight up. "Don't you bastards ever get tired?"

"Not when there's a hole as sweet as this one to be fucked Mr. Adams," Cleeve said and began thrusting hard in and out of me, getting up a good rocking rhythm on the bed.

The sounds of him spanking my ass cheeks resounded loudly in the bedroom… Otis, squatting next to my wife was teasing her hole with his fingers and the bastard was even tweaking one of her nipples under her nightgown…

"J-Justin," Linda said throatily, watching the awful spectacle as her poor husband's hole was speared again that awful night.

Cleeve rode me like a cowboy riding a wild horse in a rodeo… He reached over me, pulled my head back by a handful of my hair, kissed me hard on the mouth a couple of times and then jammed his cock real deep and real tight inside me.

"Ohhh man, feels so fucking awesome," Cleeve grunted.

It took more than a while this time for Cleeve to shoot his load. I guessed that after cumming three times it only made sense that it would take him longer this time out. But oh man, oh fucking man, how my poor hole suffered for it bud…

Ashes from Cleeve's cigar wafted down on my sweaty back as he rammed his cock in and out of me, stretching the walls of my hole more and more with each thrust. With my head down against the bed I clenched my teeth in pain and anger as the guy spanked me, pinched my ass cheeks and thrust deeper and deeper into me it seemed with each push. Then, just like the last three times he'd shot his load he jammed his monster-sized tool deep inside me, this time grabbed me by my hips and held me close to him, as he prepared to flood my hole again with his juices…

"Ohhh fuuuccckkk Otis never spewed my spunk so many times so quickly," Cleeve razzed around his cigar jammed between his back teeth. "This fucking handsome guy has got me shooting another good-sized load man!!"

He spanked my ass cheeks hard, grunted and swore like a marine and was all sweaty as he filled my crevice with his man juices.

"Ohhh yeah, nice tight shit chute you got here Justin Adams," Cleeve ranted and I felt his warm flood deep in my hole.

When he was done he slid himself out of me, climbed down off the bed after giving me a few last swats on the ass and then Otis wasted no time. Before I could even take a few breaths of relief Otis mounted the bed behind me and plunged his fat cock into my hole…

"Ohhh God!!!" I screamed my face buried in the sheets at that point.

It felt like I was being mercilessly battering rammed back there and I wondered just how much longer this would go on…

"Oh yeah Cleeve, like you said, nice tight shit chute," Otis panted as he jammed deep into my hole. "Maybe we should take this handsome guy back to the house…"

My heart thundered in more than fear at the sound of those words…

"No way Otis, we made an agreement when we found him on the train," Cleeve said with total authority. "Having snagged his home address saved us that trouble this time around…"

"Sure Cleeve, ohhh yeah, getting close already," Otis said, panting.

From what I was able to discern it was Cleeve who was in total charge of the situation here. And also from what he had said about not having to take me back to the house told me that this wasn't the first time that these two had done this sort of thing…

But then, my thoughts were cut off yet again as Otis announced that he was about to cum again…

"Ohhh man, ohhh fuckkkkk, never came so much is such a short span of time handsome guy," Otis ranted, gripping my hips tight, thrusting at what felt like lightning speed in and out of me at that point. "You have some effect on us Justin Adams…"

"S-so fucking glad to hear that you mangy bastard," I seethed into the sheets and felt Otis' slimy mess again flooding my wracked hole.

When he was done he slowly slid out of me and climbed down off the bed…

"Well, I wish that we could say we would see you again handsome guy, but obviously we couldn't risk it," Cleeve laughed as he and Otis untied my ankles from the bed, both men packed back into their jeans at that point, both of them well-spent it seemed. "A second time of this might be too much for me and Otis. Your wife and you might kill us, I mean I'm sure the two of you are wishing we'd move the fuck in here and sex you over all the time like that."

The two men laughed hysterically as Cleeve did the honors of untying my hands…

Lying there on the bed in total pain and mental anguish and

rubbing my wrists Linda and I watched as the two men exited our bedroom the same way they had entered, through the window.

"Oh God Linda, *oh my God*," I gasped and crawled down off the bed and over to her vanity table with the large mirror attached to it. "Wh-what the fuck just happened here?"

I pulled myself to a kneeling position in front of the mirror and gripping the front of the vanity with trembling hands took in the sight of my swollen and bruised face. I clenched my teeth and pain from my hole seared through me. Down on the street I heard the noise of a van pulling away...

"J-Justin pl-please," Linda whispered and I turned to look at her sitting there in tears.

I let go of the vanity and made my way over to her on my hands and knees, shaking as I went, unable to stand up straight yet. My own tears were flowing, but they were tears of rage and humiliation at what had just occurred, in my own bedroom no less.

I knelt in front of Linda and with my hands still shaking I ripped away her nightgown and plunged my tongue deep inside her, tasting Cleeve and Otis' fingers in there. I hadn't even untied her yet. As I tasted Cleeve and Otis' fingers inside my wife my cock grew hard, hard, hard... Linda threw her head back and moaned and groaned with wild abandon...

After that night Linda's and my sex life did change a little at a time. We went at it a little more ferociously at times, other times we were gentle as always. Linda found herself sliding her fingers deep into my ass hole and swirling them around in there as I would lie there jacking myself off. After I would shoot my load she went to work slurping and sucking my balls, not caring anymore how sensitive they were, torturing the very fuck out of me. I didn't protest or argue on that night she decided to tie me up and really work me over with some of the devices she had purchased in a sex shop near where she works. But good God almighty, those dildos sure can drive a guy batty; especially the battery operated ones...

The Unseen Kidnappers

"Ohhh man, you fuckin' slobs," I grunted with my head up off the table and looking down at the two men. "Fuckin' lickin' and slurpin' my damned stinking feet!! What kind of fucked up shit is that? Goddamn it you guys, but my feet stink like crazy! Why the fuck would you guys want to be lickin' and slurpin' at them? *Can't believe this shit!!*"

I lay my head back down and looked up at the ceiling as chills and goose bumps broke out all over me as the two hooded men licked and slurped at my socked feet.

"Ohhh man, ohhh fuccckkk, how'd I fall into this fucking mess?" I whispered and lay there helplessly. "God damn it, of all the fucked up things, someone fuckin' got the drop on me and kidnapped my ass!!"

I was stretched out good, rigidly and taut on my back on a solid oak table, securely strapped down with my legs spread wide and far apart. My wrists and ankles were held in place by short straps fastened to metal rings that appeared to have been hammered or soldered into the tabletop. Those rings had no length on them so moving my wrists was a total impossibility. Those, along with the heavy-duty straps pulled tightly over me kept me more than pretty much in place so that the two slobs could do their mangy work on my socked feet. Being as muscular and built like a brick shit-house like I am those straps had to be heavy-duty and pulled tighter than tight to hold me down bud. I was wearing just my nylon brown calf length dress socks; actually I had been stripped out of my brown business suit down to those socks. Fucking more than humiliating thing to happen to an executive of my stature let me tell you. The way I saw it I had been in this mess since the day before, because that was when I had worn that brown suit. I had no fucking idea where I was, why I was there, or why the two hooded men at the end of the table were delighting in licking and slurping on my strapped down brown socked and stinking feet. Actually, I stand corrected bud, it was obvious why the two bastards were delighting in licking and slurping my socked feet; *they were foot freaks, foot perverts!!* I had read about guys who were into other guy's feet and their damned smelly dress socks and sweat socks in an article about fetishism in a recent New York publication. I thought it to be kind of amusing, but not really my thing at all. I'm more into women's little pretty feet, and women's little pretty, *bare* feet. No way I would lick and slurp a woman's feet while she has her damned stockings on. And even after the times I had had some kinky fun with a couple of my girlfriend's feet they never reciprocated by servicing mine, whether I was wearing my socks or not. (This proves to me that male feet fetish is more of a guy thing, and between guys at that. Hope that makes some kind of sense bud, seeing as writing all this down is therapeutic in a way for me.) I'm the kind of guy who when he gets in bed with a girl may at times leave his socks on, only because I'm real anxious to get to her after stripping down. I never thought about it as erotic or anything like that. But now it looked like it had become my thing, or theirs to be exact. In fact, the last thing I recalled was being at work the day (night?) before. Was it the day before? Had I been here even longer than that? Now that was a scary thought! I raised my head again and looked down at the two men as they now slobbered over my socked toes and quickly sucked up their saliva. The way my nylon socks were so sopped in saliva and sweat my toes made a nice outline in them. They flicked their tongues over and over my toes, sucked my big toes one each at the same time and squeezed my arches, also at the same time. Chills coursed through me like crazy.

"*Fuck man, what is this all about???*" I asked miserably, choking back tears of humiliation mixed with rage. "Will one of you *please* answer me?"

They hunkered down at the end of the table and slowly and methodically ran their tongues up and down the bottoms of my big smelly size eleven feet. They were each wearing a leather hood. All I could see of their faces were their eyes, their nostrils, and their tongues flicking greedily over my socked feet. It was strange how the thought of when I had purchased those brown socks suddenly came to mind as the two men did their sleazy thing. It was at the same time I had bought the brown shoes in the Florsheim store right near the office building I work in, in lower Manhattan. When the salesman who had waited on me asked if I wanted to buy some socks to go with my shoes I simply said, "Yes", stating that brown and beige would be a good choice of colors for the socks. While he asked me about buying socks and while I replied the sales guy had one of my feet in hand. He seemed to be squeezing it as I reached down to get my shoes back on after having just tried on the new brown shoes. Could that salesman be one of the guys at my feet now I fleetingly wondered? I mean, it hadn't been all that long ago that I bought those shoes and socks and man, I realized now that the way he looked at me when he asked me about buying socks, it was like he was drinking in the sight of me. And he was holding one of my feet in hand at the moment. My God, I had never given any of that any thought bud…until now that is. My cock was piss hard between my legs and pointing straight up at the ceiling. I looked down at my semi hard (and getting harder) eight and a half-inch and very thick guy with a look of helplessness etched all over my square jawed face. My plum sized balls hung between my stretched legs, resting atop the table I was strapped down to. As the two men licked and slurped at the bottoms of my socked feet chills coursed through me and sped up my spine.

"Come on you guys, I think I'm entitled to some sort of an explanation here," I said pleadingly, a half grin on my face. "I mean it's not everyday that a business executive like me winds up in a position like this."

The two men stopped licking my feet for a second, looked at each other across my socked feet, and snickered meanly and fiendishly.

"He should get out more often," one of them said softly.

The other guy snapped the elastic in one of my socks against my calf and then they both resumed licking and slurping at the bottoms of my feet, slightly tickling me.

"*Shit,*" I whispered and lay my head back down again. "*Scum-bags...*"

The smell of foot sweat from my damned dress socks wafted up to my nostrils and my cock grew harder between my stretched out and strapped down tree-trunk like legs. The need to piss was excruciating but the thought of pissing on myself was more than humiliating. What fucked up irony, I thought. Humiliating to piss on myself??? What could be more humiliating than the position I was in??? Stripped to my socks and having my damned rancid feet licked and slurped by two perverts, talk about humiliating bud. Damn, where were my clothes? Where the fuck was I? What the hell was going on here??? The two men moved their mouths over my beefy heels and opened wide. They chomped on my socked heels, sending stinging pain up my spine.

"Ohhh fuck, easy you guys," I blubbered miserably. "Shit, but that hurts..."

As they mouthed my heels they ran their hands over my muscular and mighty calves, snapping the elastic in my socks against my skin again.

"*Fucking bastards,*" I ranted through clenched teeth. "Let me off this goddamned table and then we'll see just how anxious you are to suck my damned feet and play with my socks."

I wriggled my toes angrily and seemingly involuntarily under my brown nylon socks and my cock twitched hard between my legs. When the two men began sucking my socked toes pre cum oozed from my wide sexy cock slit. God, what was the story with that shit? Beads of piss mixed with my pre cum and slid down the sides of my eight and half-inch guy.

"G-God, you sleazy perverts, sucking my stinking toes," I seethed, my head raised again and looking down at the two men.

They each had the last three toes of my feet in their mouths, sucking them like crazy, squeezing my heels, making my head spin. Fuck man, I had never thought of my damned dress socks as erotic in any way. I mean I'm the type of executive dude who chooses a suit for the day makes sure the socks match and gets dressed in the morning. I don't think I'll ever look at my dress socks the same way again man. The area around the table I was on smelled of my feet sweat and the two men's saliva. Geez, talk about humiliating. Believe me I know just how bad my socks smell at the end of a long day. All I can think to do when I get them off my feet is dump them in the hamper and close it real tight. Now these two pervs were delighting in licking and sucking the smell of my rancid feet out of my socks. The two men moved to the sides of the table at my socked calves. I watched as they trailed their long mangy tongues over the sides of my socks and one of them wrapped a hand around my pulsing cock.

"Oh shit, no, *no, not this!!*" I grunted. "L-let go of me man! God almighty let go of my damned cock! I don't want a guy jacking me the fuck off. I'm no damned faggot!!"

Ignoring me, he began stroking me as they went on licking the sides of my socked calves.

"Arrrrrhhh shit, can't believe this, I-I'm going to shoot my damned load!!" I sputtered madly as the guy stroked and stroked me, my cock seeming to heat up between my legs, my big juicy balls being hefted up and down on the tabletop. "G-God, goin' to shoot my load, getting off on two pervs licking my smelly socks…"

After more than a few more good hearty strokes I spewed a real hefty executive sized mess of ball juice all over my muscular hairy chest.

"Arrrrhhh guhhhddddd…" I grunted throatily, not wanting to admit how good it actually felt as the guy stroked my mess from me.

My cum landed in rope after thick rope all over me, splattering my chest, my nipples, and stomach areas. I couldn't help but notice how some of my good stuff landed on the straps holding me tightly to the table.

"God almighty, fucking stud cums like gangbusters," one of the men said and watched through the eyeholes in his hood as I seemed to cum and cum and cum.

I grunted more than wildly and breathlessly as my cum went on and on splattering on the thick black straps holding me to the table. I writhed under those straps in a state of mixed fear and ecstasy…

"Fuck man, god damn it all, sleazy faggots got me spewing my damned executive load!!" I grunted miserably and squirmed and more than writhed at that point under the straps, my toes curling back under my socks. "Ohhh shit!!!"

Then, from behind me, after the last droplets of my mess were squeezed from me a sweet sickly scented rag was pressed firmly over my nose and mouth…

Unconsciousness claimed me and carried me off in its arms.

The next position I found myself in was worse than the one I just described. This time I found myself in a different room, hanging by my now tied wrists to an overhead pipe. The tips of my brown-socked toes were just about touching the floor. The mounds of rope around my wrists were tied more than super-tight, no way of pulling myself free. Whoever had me trapped in this godforsaken position wasn't taking any chances of me even trying to escape. As I hung there miserably feeling like a slab of beef in a butcher's freezer two more hooded men stood at my sides, their heads bent forward over my muscular chest as they slurped and sucked heartily on my silver dollar sized pink fleshy nipples.

"Arrrrrhhh shit, *what now?*" I gasped as the two men slurped at my nipples with real gusto and total zeal.

I had no idea how much time had passed since I was strapped to the table and having my socked feet licked by the two other hooded men. (How I knew that the two men slurping my nipples were not the same men who had been at my feet I did not know. Something in me, my instincts I suppose gave me this information.) I didn't know if it was the same day or days later. And of course I had no fucking idea of the identities of the two men slurping and sucking my nipples. The fact that they were hooded though told me that they didn't want me to recognize them at all, *ever*. My body was aching miserably as I hung there so I guessed that I had been strung up for quite some time. Also, I noticed that there was no caked up cum on my chest or in my chest hair. Whoever had me trapped like this had cleaned my mess off me. God, I wondered how long ago it was that I had been forced to shoot my load while strapped down to a table. I wondered how many of them it had taken to lug my ass from the room where I had been strapped down to the table to the room I was in now. A big muscular guy like me isn't some lightweight that's for fucking sure. I imagined that it had to have taken at least four of these guys to carry me to this room. Looking at the two guys feasting on my nipples I could tell that they weren't half as muscular or big as I.

"God almighty, what is this feeding time?" I asked them angrily through clenched teeth as chills and thrills sped through my entire being as they feasted and sucked my nipples. "Fuck, looks like its lunch time and my big man tits are the main fucking course! You two perverts are enjoying my man tits huh?"

For a second they stopped feasting on my nipples, looked at me, nodded "yes" and quickly slurped my big nipples back into their mangy mouths.

"Ayyyyyrrrrr shhhiiiiiitttt!!!" I ranted the feeling worse as they reclaimed my nipples into their mouths.

My nipples are more than pretty fleshy; as I said they're the size of two silver dollars on my massively muscular chest, and pink, fuck, pink as a woman's clitoris. They are surrounded on the sides by thick tufts of brown chest hair that extends out to my pecs and down to my stomach region. A hairy muscular guy, that's what the fuck I am bud. As the two men licked the tips of my nipples my cock pulsed hard and long and beefy between my aching legs. My balls hung down real low filled up again with my man juice.

"Arrrrrrrhhh God, fucking guys, goddamned perverts, making me crazy," I seethed.

As the two guys worked my nipples like crazy I recalled a date I had a while back with two, count 'em bud, *two* women. When the two women accompanied me back to my apartment after we had all met in the after work club that Friday night and they saw the size of my nipples after I took off the top portion of my suit they nearly went crazy with hunger. Standing there I had all to do to balance myself on my feet as they each slurped and daintily sucked at my big man tits. They stretched me out on my bed in just my under shorts with my cock sticking out of them and took turns jacking me off, seeing how many times they could make me cum while they went on and on working my nipples. And that was just the foreplay that night bud. But now, two guys, no, fuck that, two perverts were working my man tits, and I had a hard on no less??? What was up with all this shit? The two men ran their hands over me as they went on and on feasting heartily at my poor nipples. They weren't gentle and dainty the way my two female dates had been that night. They caressed and slapped my stomach and chest and pecs areas, fingered my bushy armpits, and reached around me to steal squeezes off my tight round buns.

"Errrrhhh!!!" I really seethed now. *Faggots, that's what the fuck you all are, goddamned faggots!!* Get your mangy hands off me!!"

With their hands squeezing my butt cheeks real hard and the way they were really putting the screws to my nipples at that point made me buck my muscular body forward. I stood there now in a sort of arched position with just the tips of my socked toes barely touching the floor.

"Ayyyyyyyy, you bastards," I said in a high-pitched tone of voice.

The sounds of slurping and sucking filled my ears and chills more than sped through me and a long while later they were still at it. At that point my nipples were sore, numb and tingling. They sucked the thick hair on the sides of my nipples in between slurps and licks at my man tits, really causing me pain when they did that. After a few seconds of sucking my thick hair tufts with their lips they would quickly slurp my poor nipples back into their greedy mouths.

"Ayyyyrrrrr shhhiiiittt," I seethed in pain every time they reclaimed my man tits into their mouths.

I wriggled around on my toes as the two men ate and ate my nipples…

"Say guys, how about giving those man tits of mine a break huh?" I asked them, trying to sound friendly.

In response I received two hard open-handed slaps on my stomach region.

"Owwwwwwwwww!!! Well, so much for that request," I muttered miserably.

I looked up at my bound wrists and again wondered desperately how I had gotten into this mess. I tried so hard to recall the last normal moment on my workday before finding myself the way I was now, stripped to my damned stinking dress socks and being used as a sex toy. I saw myself sitting at my desk at the bank I work for as a loan officer. I saw myself signing papers, authorizing transactions, and answering phones. I recalled a stressful workday. I recalled someone telling me that I needed to relax that I needed a vacation. But then my thoughts were rudely interrupted by a hard slap administered to my firm ass as the two men went on working my poor nipples.

"Owwwwww shit!!!" I roared angrily.

When they finally stopped eating my nipples the poor nubs were swollen to the size of two ripe cherries. The tips of them were more than hard and super erect. The two men touched them lightly with the tip of their fingers.

"Ohhh fuckers, look what the hell you two did to my damned man tits," I said, twisting myself around slightly, wanting more than anything to have my hands free just for a moment, God; just for a moment bud and I would pummel the two tit eaters.

Snickering, each of the men took a clip-on clothespin from their pants pockets.

"Oh no, no," I pleaded, trying totally desperately to back away from the two men as they squeezed the clothespins open. "Y-you bastards, *you wouldn't, you wouldn't, not after you just made my poor man tits all sensitive…*"

But alas, they did, and in the worst possible way at that. They clipped the clothespins right onto the very erect, very sensitive tips of my poor over-worked nipples.

"AYYYYYYRRRRR!!!" I roared in a man's agony, an agony I never knew before, twisting and writhing miserably in the bondage.

As I hung there sputtering and gasping in stinging pain one of the men grabbed my hard and pulsing eight and a half-inch guy. The need to piss was beyond excruciating now and I was harder than when I had been strapped down to the table in the other room.

"Ohhh no, no, not this shit again too!!" I blubbered crazily as the guy began stroking me. "Oh God, this isn't going to take long."

So true, after a few good hearty strokes the bastard had me spewing another hefty sized mess of thick creamy executive spunk.

"Ayyyyyrrrrrrr fuck, fucking perverts, sleazy bastards," I grunted through clenched teeth, my hands balled tight into a big fist above me, standing there on my toes as I shot my load and shot my load.

I felt it like crazy in my clothes-pinned man tits, the numb tingling sensation searing through them as I was milked… Then, looking downward I watched as my spunk flew and erupted from me in ropes, landing on the floor more than a few feet away from me. As I spewed my mess of ball juice the pain in my nipples intensified more than one hundred percent. Fuck, I had just learned that when a guy shoots his load while his man tits are clipped or clamped they become more than super duper sensitive…

"AYYYYYRRRRRR shhhiiiiitttttt," I panted as giant goose bumps popped up and rippled all over my well-toned muscular body.

My nipples were beyond sensitive as I shot my load and shot my load and fucking shot my load…

"Ohhh fuck," I grunted as the last droplets of my ball juice hit the floor, and as I was forced through this torturous ecstasy.

The guy then let go of my cock and as the clothespins were taken off my nipples a white cloth was again pressed over my nose and mouth from behind me... The sweet sickly smell turned my thoughts to fuzz and once again sleep claimed me...

As I slept I either dreamed or recalled the last morning I was at home living a normal guy's life. Like any other workday the alarm clock rang, jarring me from sleep. I rubbed my eyes, climbed out of bed, and padded in just my boxer shorts in the dark to the bathroom. I've been living in my apartment so long now that walking in the dark from my bedroom to the bathroom is no difficult chore whatsoever. In the bathroom I flicked on the light, allowed my eyes to adjust to the fluorescent glare and then positioned myself over the toilet bowl. My thick, eight and a half inch guy (that's what I call my cock) was hard as a fucking rock and pulsing (as usual.) Standing over the bowl I pushed my boxer shorts off myself, kicked them aside, and grabbed my erection.

"Ohhh yeah, fucking A," I grunted in an early morning throaty sounding voice.

Standing there in my naked and musculature glory I stroked myself slowly, cupped my plum sized balls in my other hand and gently squeezed them.

"Mmmmmm yeah," I crooned with my eyes now closed.

I rocked back and forth on my big size eleven feet, stroking myself a little faster with each beat. I thought about Linda, the girl I have been seeing lately. I thought about Ruth, who works in the Credit department at the bank I work for. I thought about the girl whose name I didn't know that I saw on the train each morning with her husband. (boyfriend?) I squeezed my nuts a little more and then I felt it, I was about to spew a good-sized load of morning creamy ball juice. I opened my eyes, stroked my thick long meat a little more, and aimed it at the toilet bowl. I erupted with a morning geyser of cum, gushing into the bowl.

"Ohhh yeah, fucking A!!" I grunted letting go of my balls and letting them swing freely as ropes and ropes of my good stuff landed in the toilet, making a plopping sound each time in the water. "Great fucking way to start the day!! *Oh fuck yeah!!*"

When I was done I squeezed the last droplets of cum from my

slit and then remained standing there, catching my breath. I then pissed a heavy-duty sized stream of yellow man juice into the bowl.

"Oooooooo yeah, really drainin' the vein this morning," I grunted and ran a hand through my sleep mussed hair.

My pissing seemed to go on and on, just as it seems to go on and on when I shoot my load. I often wonder if all muscular guys like me are like that. When I was done pissing the sour scent of my yellow stream wafted up at me. I flushed the toilet and stepped over to the bathtub. I turned on the water faucets for a morning shower, standing there as the water warmed up to my satisfaction. Waiting for the water to adjust I glanced at my reflection in the full-length mirror. I'm six feet four inches tall, I have short cut black silky hair, dark marble shaped eyes, and my body is well toned and more than muscular. Fuck man, I'm built like a goddamned brick shit house. Not an ounce of fat on me thanks to a healthy diet and a regular exercise regimen. Damn, fists as big as hams, arms wiry and mounded with biceps the size of bowling balls, shoulders as wide as a goddamned doorway. And that stomach area, fucking six pack buds and hard as a brick wall. I stepped into the shower and let the warm water cascade over me, soak me before lathering up. My chest is also extremely wide and muscular, bouncing pecs I got bud (about forty to forty two inches across give or take an inch) and hairy, hairy like a goddamned gorilla. As I said earlier, a real hairy muscular guy, that's what the fuck I am. (Vulgar too I suppose it could be said.) As I stood there under the warm flowing water my cock grew hard again. Grinning snidely I reached for the soap and began lathering myself up.

"Fuck guy, always hard as a fucking rock," I said to my big cock. "No wonder Linda loves you so much."

I chuckled happily and soaped myself all over, talking to my cock, what a hoot. I had every reason in the world to chuckle happily. I was a successful businessman with a top-notch bank. I'm a loan officer at the age of twenty-six, one of the youngest executives to ever reach that status. I worked hard to get to where I am, putting in long hours, Saturdays, and not to mention the four years of college to earn my degree. Successful, that's a good word to describe me. Good old happy successful Joe Griffin. When I was done I emerged from the shower feeling refreshed and wide-awake, ready to tackle the day ahead of me. I towel dried and then, standing naked in front of the sink I brushed my teeth. Back in my bedroom I dressed for the day in a brown suit, white button down shirt, beige silk tie, brown calf length nylon socks, and brown slip-on shoes. As I rolled my socks onto my feet that morning I had no idea, not the slightest inkling that I would find myself strapped to a table and having my socked feet licked and slurped by two foot perverts. Hell, when I rolled my socks on that morning I didn't have the slightest clue that I would find myself stripped to them and being used as a sex toy... Fully dressed, I picked up my briefcase and left my apartment...

The smell of soap filled my nostrils as I came to sitting on my knees. As I slowly came around the first thing I realized was that my hands were now roped tightly behind me at the wrists. As my vision cleared and I looked around I saw that I was in a bathroom. And not just any bathroom let me tell you, but a beautiful and huge state of the art bathroom.

"Shit, where the fuck am I?" I said softly, still looking around the beige and cream-colored bathroom.

I was kneeling against a gleaming clean toilet, which was how I had been positioned in the bathroom on my knees. Next to the toilet was a large vanity and sink. On the other side of the bathroom was a huge round tub with three showerheads over the top of it. With my lips trembling I pulled myself to my socked feet. The immaculately clean tile floor felt cool through my thin socks.

"Wh-where the fuck am I?" I whispered desperately. "*What is this place?*"

When this had all first started I imagined I was dreaming. But looking around the bathroom, the feeling of soreness in my cock and man tits and the cool tile floor under my socked feet all attested to the fact that I was wide awake...at least at that moment I was...

Over the sink was a large mirrored medicine cabinet. Scotch taped to the mirror was a sheet of paper with writing on it. When I saw that the opening words on the paper read "Dear Mr. Griffin" I nearly jumped out of my damned smelly socks. Standing there feeling totally helpless I read the letter. If memory serves me correctly it read almost exactly as follows:

Dear Mr. Griffin,

First and foremost we want to suggest that you use your limited time in the bathroom wisely. In other words, piss!! Relieve yourself. You have been with us for a day and a half now. We are sure that the need to piss must me maddening for you at this point. You will be fed a hearty meal tonight. We will not let you starve. You may consider yourself our guest here, our captive guest if you would. You will not be permanently damaged whatsoever. You will not be kept for longer than necessary. And you will not be told where you are or who we are. Usually we will allow our guests to know us, see us, talk with us, but in your case we do need to make a definite exception in those areas. You will obey any and all wishes of our clients when they visit their advances upon you and your person. As you have come to know already we have very interesting, eccentric and exciting clients. Your feet and nipples should be feeling pretty good at this point. There is more to come. We can't promise that all our clients will be as gentle and sensual as these men were so you best prepare yourself for some nastiness. The method used to render you unconscious is an old and simple one, chloroform. It is what was used when we managed to so cleverly nab you and spirit you off here. Please know that not just any man is chosen to be in the position you are currently in Mr. Griffin. We carefully search out and seek only the most handsome, most muscular, most virile appearing and most noble of sorts. You should feel honored that you were hand picked by us. The combination of your rugged yet dignified good looks and above average height was what drew you to our decision and us. May we welcome you and also tell you that we were not disappointed with your meat department. We are looking forward to seeing just how many loads you can produce and spurt for us. Realizing just how potent you are is the key reason we need to keep your hands tied and away from your eight and a half inch guy, as you so aptly call that meat stick of yours. Your loads of mess and good stuff will be saved for and extracted only by our clients. Now, for the moment, go and piss. Feel the relief of pissing after having not for more than a day or so. When you are done you will kneel back against the toilet in the position you found yourself in when you awoke. You will face forward and remain that way no matter what transpires. Failure to follow any and all directions will be dealt with most severely Mr. Griffin.

Sincerely, C & O.

For whatever the fuck the reason those two initials C & O looked somewhat familiar but I could not at the moment think why. I glanced down at my nipples and saw that they had returned to a somewhat normal look. I was still able to smell the men's saliva on my socks mixed with the pungent odor of my feet sweat. I released a long held breath and walked slowly over to the toilet. My soft, more than piss filled cock dangled and swung between my legs. What they had said in their letter was true; the need to piss was maddening. Had I really not pissed since the day before all this started? I positioned myself over the toilet and pissed and pissed, long and hard. Relief filled me.

"Ahhh!!!" I sighed loudly. "Fuckin' pissin' real thick lemonade…"

As I stood there pissing and pissing one word from the letter I had just read kept going creepily through my mind. Clients. Their clients. *Clients???* I was obviously being used as some sort of twisted combination of a sex slave and prostitute, although in the case of a guy it would be called a hustler. Only the money was not going into my pockets. Utter rage coursed through me at what felt like a hundred fucking miles per hour.

"Grrrrrrrr!!!" I seethed through clenched teeth and tried desperately to get my hands untied.

No use though, my hands were tied too fucking tight. Strong and stalwart as I am there was no way I was getting out of those damned ropes bud. When I was (finally) done pissing I stood there feeling somewhat relieved yet totally terrified at the same time. There was no way to flush the toilet and the sour scent of my piss wafted up to me from the bowl. Also in the letter scotch taped to the mirror they said that they usually, *usually* allow their so-called guests to see them know them, talk with them, but in my case they had to make a definite exception. Why? *Why?* Did I know these people? Did they know me? Was that why they needed to keep their identities hidden from me? Slowly and miserably I lowered myself to my knees in front of the toilet, knowing all too well what was going to happen next. Chloroform, it was what was used when they (whoever *they were*) managed to nab me. But nab me from where? And when??? According to the letter on the mirror I had been there for a day and a half now. I could not recall being chloroformed on that last day at work. My thoughts were cut off when I heard the bathroom door opening behind me. My breath came in gasps as I heard footsteps approaching me from behind. My heart raced in total and paralyzing fear. Then, the chloroform soaked cloth was pressed firmly over my nose and mouth. I tried to hold my breath but it was no use. I took a needed breath and fell into a more than sleepy stupor. I heard the sound of the toilet flushing and then felt myself being lifted. Good God, I was being lifted by one guy bud, stronger than strong fucker he had to be. I was carried out of the bathroom the way a bridegroom would carry his bride over a threshold. The last thought I had before completely losing consciousness was that this guy (whoever he was) had to be super duper fucking strong in order to hoist me this way...

"Ohhh God," I seethed miserably and angrily through clenched teeth. "Of all the fucked up things, *I cannot believe this has happened to me!!*"

I was standing on the side of the large table I had been strapped down to. This time my arms were spread out wide and tied off at the wrists tightly to the rings that were at the ends of the table. The table was bolted to the floor I noticed as I struggled in vain. My socked feet were spread wide as well and tied off at the ankles to the legs of the table, exposing my pink raunchy virgin bunghole. A cock ring was snapped tightly around the base of my cock and balls, keeping me hard as a fucking rock and driving me crazy with pain at the same time. (Fuck, they didn't need to clip that cock ring onto me to keep me hard bud. Good ol' Joe Griffin is a twenty-four hour a day hard-on.) Beads upon beads of pre cum seeped and oozed from my wide sexy slit under the table. Not being able to get to my cock and relieve myself was maddening, even though I was in pain at the same time. A pair of metal and heavy ball bearings attached to strings was tied onto my big juicy and luscious balls, torturing the fuck out of my poor testicles. They dangled just above the floor, those metal fuckers, pulling hard on my poor balls.

"Grrrrrrrr!!! What a fucked up position to be in!!" I ranted, trying desperately to get myself untied.

I didn't need three guesses to know what was going to happen next. I was about to be fucked in the ass like a goddamned whore. I tottered on my tied, socked feet and the ball bearings on my nuts tugged them down even more.

"ARRRRRRRHHH Shit!" I grunted.

Then, the door to the room I was in opened and then closed behind me. Footsteps approached me from behind.

"*Oh no, no,*" I whispered, beginning to sweat in total fear.

Shit, just the thought of having my bunghole reamed was too much to think about bud. Two men stepped to my sides. Like the others before them they were hooded. Only their eyes, nostrils, and mouths were visible to me. They stood at my sides and ran their hands over me, exploring me, squeezing me, getting to know me so to speak.

"Bastards, get your paws off me!!" I reeled as their hands moved over my hairy butt cheeks. "I'm no sick perverted faggot!!"

They squeezed my butt cheeks and tweaked my nipples hard at the same time, twirling their fingers on them. A wave of dizziness consumed me and I leaned my head back, looking up at the ceiling.

"G-God, shitty thing to have happened to a guy like me," I muttered and then to my utter shock and dismay one of the men clamped his mouth down on mine.

"RRRRRmmmmffffff!!!" I sputtered madly as his tongue invaded my mouth.

Now, just for the record here *I am not gay* and had never kissed a guy before that. Shit, I had never even entertained thoughts of kissing a guy before in my life. As the guy forced his tongue deeper into my craw I tasted cigars and his buddy stuck a finger (or two) into my virgin hole. If my feet hadn't been tied at the ankles to that table I would have jumped right the fuck out of my socks. Having your hole prodded can really have that effect on a guy let me tell you. The guy's finger probed deep in my hole, prodding me, exploring me back there, sending pain and chills through me. The way his finger dug in my hole it was like he was searching for buried treasure back there or something.

"We're going to have to lube this slab of beef real well," I heard the guy say and his buddy kissed me harder, really pressing his lips against mine. (Fucker, referring to me as a slab of beef made me feel less than human…)

To my further shock I found myself responding to the other guy's kiss, snaking my tongue into his mouth, sucking his tongue, and pressing my trembling lips hard against his. When he stopped kissing me I could tell that he was smiling maniacally behind his hood.

"Yeah, let's lube this handsome dude," he said in a very macho sounding voice.

He leaned down and with the tips of his fingers gave my dangling balls a light slap.

"YAHHH!!!" I cried out miserably and in pain.

I saw stars for a few seconds and then the two men were hunkered down at my ass cheeks. They ran their big hands over my ass, pulled a few strands of hair out of my butt cheeks just to make me squeal, and teased my hole with their fingers. Squatting there they also ran their hands up and down my strong muscular legs, toying with my socks, snapping them against my legs.

"Bastards," I seethed miserably and wriggled my toes angrily under my socks. "What the fuck is it with all you perverts and my damned socks?"

"Real nice hole he has eh?" the guy with the macho sounding voice asked his buddy.

"Yeah, real nice, lets get it all juicy," the other guy said in a husky tone of voice.

They began taking turns spitting into my hole. The first time the guy with the macho sounding voice spewed a wad of saliva into my hole my eyes opened wide in shock and total distress and my head popped up rapidly. I could not believe this shit. Never before had my hole been used in this fashion. Their warm and soupy saliva drenched my hole and made it feel all slick and sopped back there. In between spits they prodded my hole with their fingers, sticking two and three digits in there at once. They dug deep bud; causing me a pain I had never known before. They spit into my hole a few more times each.

"Let me really get him moist," one of them said and then pressed his face against my raunchy crack.

His tongue snaked deeply into my hole and he dribbled saliva in there, and then he began flicking his tongue over my bung.

"Ohhh God," I grunted throatily. "Fucking pervert, *degenerate!!* You bastard, eating and munching on my damned hole!!"

As he squatted there delighting in eating my stink hole his buddy stood up at my side and leered meanly at me from behind his hood. His eyes looked filled with raw and primitive lust. He leaned in and grabbed one of my big nipples between his thumbs and first two fingers.

"Nice tits you got guy," he said tauntingly and gave it a hard squeeze followed by a twist.

I looked at him with utter hatred in my eyes as he teased and squeezed the fuck out of my man tit.

"Okay, he's ready and primed," the other guy said when he'd had enough of eating and dribbling in my hole.

He stood up at my other side. I watched as the two men pulled down the zippers of their jeans and brought out their long, hard, thick and pulsing tube steaks.

"*Oh fuck, no, no,*" I said in a high-pitched tone of voice, choking back tears. "Please guys, *not this!!*"

But, to my dismay I saw that my pleading only turned them on all the more and drove them. As I shook and trembled in the bondage the guy with the bigger cock took position behind me. He grabbed me by my hips and slowly began pushing his hardness into my hole.

"Ooooooo sh-shit," I moaned when the crown of his cock was in my hole.

He thrust in and out a little bit; entering me a little more each time he went back in. His cock felt like it was teasing my bung. He ran his hands up and down my hips, caressing me as he entered me inch by blasted inch.

"Arrrrrrrrhhh shit, you fuckers," I muttered and clenched my bound hands into big fists. "Fucking bastards, you sick fucks, untie me and then we'll see just how anxious you are to fuck my damned hole!! I swear to God I'll make short work of both of you at the same goddamned time!!"

As the first guy moved his cock further and further into my hole with each thrust the other guy stood at my side tweaking and twirling his fingers over one of my nipples. Goose bumps broke out all over my body, I was sweating like crazy, and the stink of my socks was awful at that point. Then, the guy fucking me rammed his cock all the way in.

"AYYYYYYRRRRR!!!" I roared in a totally new pain, something that I had never experienced before. "Ohhh good Gods, you miserable bastards!!!"

He pulled his cock halfway out and thrust back in again, deeper this time, ramming me hard a second time.

"Ayyyyyyyyyyyyyyyrrrrr!!!" I screamed again, louder this time.

"Oh man, this guy has some hole, nice and tight and fucking squishy in there," the guy fucking the tar out of me said to his buddy and pressed himself up against my rippled and muscular back.

His cock was wedged deep in my hole now and driving me batty. He thrust only slightly out and rammed back in again and again, his cock seeming to not want to leave the tight confines of my hole. The guy kissed the back of my big neck and ran his tongue over it, slobbering over me as he fucked me and fucked me and fucked me hard some more.

"Ohhh you scumbag!!" I grunted as he nipped at one of my earlobes.

All the while though my cock remained hard and at attention under the table, my poor balls dangling painfully low because of those damned ball bearings tied to them along with the cock ring clipped onto them. God, with that damned cock ring on me there was no way my cock was going to go down. Whoever had kidnapped my handsome ass wanted to make sure of that bud. As the other guy teased and teased my nipple my cock twitched long and hard under the table, *needing* release now.

"Ohhh man, I'm goin' to shoot my load man!!" the guy fucking me panted and gave one of my butt cheeks a hard slap.

"Owwwwwww!!" I bellowed.

He pulled his cock out of my hole and grabbed it in his hand, aiming the thing at my back. I felt his hot load land in big thick ropes all over my big muscular back.

"Ohhh yeah, great looking dude you are guy," he said breathlessly, spurting his mess all over my back. "Great thing to have fucked the bejesus out of you. Ohhh fuck yeah…"

"Fucking mangy bastard, don't need your sticky stuff all over me man," I grunted angrily, feeling defiled as he spurted his cum on me.

He seemed to cum and cum, drenching my back with his juices. It slid down my spine and into the crack of my ass. My hole was still hurting and twitching from the beating it had just taken. How I wished I could give a beating of my own at that moment let me tell you. Fucking a guy's hole, damn, the very gall of these guys… When the first guy was done shooting his load the second guy let go of my nipple. Looking at me from the side he grinned meanly behind his hood and said "My turn."

"Oh no, no, not again," I muttered more than angrily as he took position behind me.

Like his buddy he grabbed my hips, but unlike his buddy he didn't enter me a little at a time. Instead he rammed me good and hard, anxious to get his big pulsing tool deep inside me.

"Ohhh SHIT, SHIT," I panted miserably in pain and threw my head back on his shoulder.

He leaned into me and kissed my lips as he fucked me hard and callously. Once again I surprised myself by responding to his kiss, snaking my tongue into his mouth.

"Ha!!!" he laughed and thrust in and out of my poor hole. "I think this fucking guy is in love with me!! Second fucking time he kissed me."

His buddy watched as he fucked me and fucked me, his cock getting hard again. I looked over at him in horror.

"Ha, ha, that's right handsome guy," the first guy said to me tauntingly. "I'm going to have another good go at that sweet hole of yours!!"

"Ohhh NO, NO, y-you sick fucks!!" I ranted as the second guy slapped my butt cheeks hard and fucked me like crazy.

"Ohhh yeah, now I'm getting close you handsome fuck!!" the second guy muttered breathlessly in my ear, his tongue lapping at my earlobe.

Unlike his buddy he didn't pull out of me before shooting his load. He kept his cock wedged tightly in my hole and I felt his hot juices flood me.

"Ohhh yeahhh, yeah!!" he seethed, grabbing my upper arms in a tight grip, kneading and squeezing my huge biceps, thrusting in and out of my hole as he came and came. "Fucking gorgeous bastard you are guy."

When he was done shooting his load he kept his softening cock inside me and held me tighter and tighter by my upper muscular biceps. He moved in close to me and again planted a hard kiss on my lips. He wasn't out of my hole for more than fifteen seconds and his buddy was inside me again for another round of fucking me long and hard.

"Ohhh man, ohhh fuckkkk, great fucking hole you got here Stud!!" the first guy grunted as he slid into my sopped up crevice and rammed me and rammed me. "I could more than likely fuck you all day long, and then all night long, but that would probably cost extra!!"

At that remark the two men snickered meanly and tauntingly.

The guy fucking me slapped my butt cheeks hard and pulled more hairs out of them.

"Yarrrrrrhhh!!!" I gasped loudly. "Shit, but that hurts!!"

By the time it was over the two men had fucked me three times each. I couldn't believe their stamina. My poor hole was aching and sopping wet with their juices as they packed their spent cocks back into their pants and zipped up.

"Oh man, that was great guy," the first guy said and gave one of my butt cheeks a hard squeeze.

"Gl-glad you enjoyed it, so glad I could be of service," I muttered angrily and sarcastically.

"Oh, don't forget to blindfold him before we walk out of here," the second guy said in reminder to his buddy. "Yeah, they don't want him seeing anyone when they come in to knock him out."

I sighed miserably as one of the men tied a white cloth blindfold over my eyes.

"Man, I wouldn't want to be in your shoes, or socks right now Stud," the guy snickered as he blindfolded me.

I heard the door to the room open as they left. My cock twitched long, hard and painfully under the table. Then, a chloroform soaked cloth was *again* pressed firmly against my nose and mouth. I was asleep in seconds…

As I slept off the latest dose of chloroform I had been dealt I again dreamed (or somehow in my sleep recalled) of the last normal day of my life. After having left my apartment I walked the few blocks to the train station. It was a cool early spring morning and the sun was just rising as I walked. I waited the usual few minutes for the "B" train to arrive at the eighteenth avenue train station. The usual morning crowd was all there. The young construction worker with the older guy that he rides with everyday was there. The Old Italian guy, who is married but always rides with this really young pretty girl, I know he wants to fuck the shit out of her, and if she gave him a green light I'm sure he would not hesitate. The two middle aged Russian guys were there too, construction workers I think they are. Actually, I'm the only suit on the train at that time of the morning. Mostly blue-collar workers ride the train that early in the morning. When the train arrived at the usual time I boarded and sat down in my usual seat. Sitting across from me was the guy who is always reading a book. He looks to be in his mid thirties. He has short cut brown hair and deep brown eyes. He is always dressed in casual office attire. As I pulled an exercise magazine from my briefcase I saw him steal a glance at me. I always had the feeling that he was gay, but in all honesty it didn't bother me. If the guy got his rocks off checking me out during his ride to work so be it. Live and let live and all that shit you know. I was secured enough with whom I was not to worry about it. Not to mention that it gave me a creepy kind of thrill knowing that the faggot was turned on by me. Now, however, I was no longer so secured in who I was, seeing as I had become a sex slave of sorts for someone (more than one person?) and had no idea if I would ever know a normal life again. At the station where I make a connection to a local train I disembarked from the "B" train. The guy reading his book stole a last glance at me as I walked off the train as he remains on the train after I get off. As I came to I wondered if one of those people that I see every morning on the train had anything to do with the situation I was in now...

"Ohhhrrrr man, fucking sleaze bags, fuckers, sucking my eight and a half inch guy," I blubbered, roped tightly to a pole and sweating, all smelly and randy at that point. "Never had any fucking *guys* suck my meat before!!"

I had found myself this time roped tightly to a post in the center of yet another room when I had come to again. What kind of place (house) was this with so many rooms in it? My arms were pulled back around the big structure and my upper muscular body was tightly roped to it, fastening me in place. The ropes were tied over and under my massive pecs, making a real nice showcase of my big nipples. My legs, like my arms were pulled back around the post so that I was standing just about on my damned socked toes. Rope was tied around my thick muscled thighs and the back of it was tied off to the ropes around my chest. What a miserable and fucked up position to be in!! As I came to I felt a tingling sensation in my soft cock. When I opened my eyes I saw that there were two new hooded men squatting at my crotch. The bastards, the sleazy faggots, they were taking turns sucking my soft cock, twirling it around with their fingers, and tugging on my big smelly balls. The cock ring and ball bearings were off me at that point, thank God! When I came to one of the guys said that he was glad to see me awake, adding that maybe now my cock would get hard. I wondered how long I had been roped up to the post and how long the two perverts had been at my cock and balls. They ran their goddamned hands up and down my tied up muscular legs, playfully snapped the elastic in my socks against my calves, and slurped heartily at my soft cock.

"Perverts!! Fucking bastards!!" I roared down at them as I slowly opened my eyes. "Wh-what kind of men are you that you would suck another guy's cock with such gusto?"

"Ah, maybe now we'll get somewhere and see just how many loads this muscle boy can cook up for us," the guy squatting at my right said happily.

When they each slurped one of my balls into their mouths I nearly jumped out of my damned stinking socks.

"Yarrrrhhh God!!!" I roared mightily, my deep voice echoing and bouncing off the walls. "Ohhh my poor balls!"

Now I know that most guys out there enjoy having their family jewels licked, sucked, and oh God, even chewed on, *but not me.* No fucking way man, not handsome Joe Griffin, my balls are super sensitive to the touch. The way the two guys were sucking on them, pulling on them with their lips, and slurping the fuck out of them was driving me crazy with pain. I balled my hands into tight fists and clenched my teeth.

"G-God almighty, you fucking bastards, you buckets of scum," I seethed as spittle flew out of my mouth. "I swear to God, if I get myself untied you faggots will be history!!"

Then, the guy on my right stopped sucking my testicle that was in his mouth and slurped my eight and a half inch guy into it.

"Yuhhh!!!" I gasped and slammed my head back against the post I was roped to. "F-fucker, suckin' my cock again!!"

Being that I was now totally conscious I had no problem getting a cock stand for the two perverts as they worked my eight and a half inch guy and balls with real gusto, torturing me with pleasure and pain at the same fucking time. As the guy on my right sucked me up to a big old hard-on the guy on my left continued sucking and slurping at my testicle in his mouth. I was in a mixture of ecstasy and outright torture all at once; a lot to think about bud let me tell you. When I was good and more than hard and pulsing in the guy on my right's mouth I felt it.

"Ohhh you fuckers, you goddamned perverts," I grunted, feeling totally humiliated. "I-I'm goin' to shoot my goddamned load!!"

The guy sucking my cock sucked me faster and faster.

"Ohhh shhhiiiittt," I seethed and erupted like a volcano in his greedy mouth. "YEAHHH!!!"

I came like gangbusters, filling and filling the pervert's mouth with it as his buddy went on and on sucking, slurping and chomping at my testicle that was in his mouth.

"AYYYYYYYRRRR, greedy bastard, eatin' my good stuff!" I roared, looking down at the guy as he swallowed my load. "Goddamned fucker, chowing down on my executive jizz!! Pervert!!"

He swallowed just about every drop of my creamy and thick sperm. What he couldn't swallow oozed out of the sides of his mouth and dripped to the floor. I grunted and groaned like a fucking soldier as the bastard forced every possible drop out of me. When I was done shooting my load the bastard didn't let my cock out of his mouth. Instead, he just kept on sucking and sucking me. It seemed that my ranting, swearing and cursing at the two perverts just drove them on all the more. I wondered if when they had paid to use me if they had specifically requested a dude that would use derogatory words and phrases on them.

"Ohhh no, *no*," I panted. *"Come on man, ohhh G-God, I-I'm all sensitive and sexy feeling after I've shot a good sized load of soup!!"*

But the two men were more than relentless, more than persistent bud. They again took turns slurping my cock in and out of their mouths. They took turns holding my cock tight and poking the tips of their tongues into my above average sized slit. (That really sent chills through me let me tell you!) They drove me nearly insane with pleasure sucking on just the crown of my slimy and saliva soaked eight and a half inch guy. Shit, I hadn't even had a chance to get soft and shriveled after having shot my load. Fucking perverted guys just went on and on working my poor cock and balls.

"Ohhh you fuckers," I groaned throatily, feeling myself getting ready to shoot a second load for them, a true victim of their sleazy handiwork. "Goin' to have me cumming again so fucking soon!!"

As one of the men held my pulsing and sore cock in his fist I shot a second load onto the floor in front of me.

"OHHH!!!" I roared breathlessly, goose bumps breaking out all over me as I spewed and spewed my sexy mess.

The guy holding my eight and a half inch guy stroked me like crazy as the other guy tugged hard on my aching balls.

"AYYYYRRRRR!!!" I squeaked as the last droplets of sperm oozed from my wide sexy slit.

"Now we're really going to have him going crazy," the guy on my right said gleefully and slurped my semi hard cock into his mouth.

"OOOOOOOOOOOOOOO," I gasped, my mouth open wide in a big "O" shape, my eyes crossing in my head.

"No, oh no," I pleaded as the room spun in front of me.

Now I knew what they had meant when one of them had talked about finding out how many loads I could cook up for them. These guys were the types who got their rocks off making a big dude like me shoot his load for them. My poor numb cock tingled miserably in the guy's mouth as he sucked it more than heartily. The other guy went for my balls again, running his hand up and down my leg, snapping the elastic in my sock against my calf. I panted frantically for breath and I was sweating like a pig and totally stinking of it all by then.

"OHHH!!!" I roared in the throes of forced ecstasy.

It took more than a while, but God almighty, it seemed that those two just loved sucking my cock and chomping on my big smelly balls, but I did shoot a third load for them. They must have been cock and balls magicians I thought fleetingly. Actually, it was just a small spurt of cum that erupted from my cock and into the pervert's mouth that time. And after that they forced me to *still* cum some more. I was beyond sensitized after a while and it seemed that my orgasms just erupted from me one after the other. I lost count of how many climaxes they squeezed out of me but then after a while I was suffering what was called dry orgasms. And *that* nearly did drive me utterly crazy. I would think that that would drive most guys eventually over the edge. Feeling myself having an orgasm, climaxing, chills and thrills enveloping me, but nothing shooting from my cock was utter and total insanity. Chloroform was not needed to render me unconscious that time. As I suffered what must have been the umpteenth cock eruption I passed out cold…

The aromas of good food filled the air. I quickly thought that I was in a ritzy restaurant on lunch hour having a business meeting. But alas, as I came to I recalled miserably where I really was at that moment, in the clutches of some unseen kidnappers. I was seated on a soft cushioned chair, my hands securely tied at the wrists behind me, the slack of the rope tied off to the back of the chair. I however could not see shit as delicious food was put into my mouth because *I was blindfolded. Fuck!!* I sat there in just my damned stinking socks being fed what tasted like delicious stir-fried chicken, stewed tomatoes, baked potatoes, and I was made to sip cold mineral water through a straw. As I chewed mouthfuls of food I heard other sounds of chewing nearby me. More than likely my captors, my blasted hosts if you would were having their dinner as well. I guessed it to be evening as I sat there tied and blindfolded, being fed like a fucking baby. I knew better than to ask where I was, who my kidnappers were, or how much longer I would be held there. From the note I had read while in the bathroom I knew that it would be fruitless to ask anything. I mean fuck, even the men who'd had their sick ways with me wouldn't tell me shit. As I ate I tried desperately to think about what I had come to call the last normal day of my life…

After switching from the express "B" train to the local "R" train at the Pacific Street station in Brooklyn I rode to Wall Street in Manhattan where I disembarked the train. I tossed my exercise magazine in a trash bin and headed for the coffee shop that I go to every morning religiously. The young guy, who works behind the counter of the coffee shop didn't have to ask me anything as he filled a large Styrofoam cup with freshly brewed coffee. He put one sweet and low and low fat milk in it for me, bagged it and said good morning to me as I handed him two dollars. His hand lightly brushed mine as he took my money from me. I said, "good morning" to him as he dropped a few coins in my hand, change. With my coffee in hand I left the shop and made my way to my office. Shit, could the guy who serves me my coffee every morning have been the one who kidnapped me? Or maybe it was that gay guy on the train, or maybe, maybe, *maybe*. Shit, this was becoming too much. I rode the elevator to the floor that I work on in the big Wall Street building that the bank I work for is housed in. When I got to my desk I instantly booted up my computer, took my coffee out of the bag, took the lid off it, and shucked off my suit jacket, hanging it neatly on the back of my chair. I sat down. As my computer booted up I took a low fat cereal bar from my top desk drawer and peeled the foil wrapper off it. I popped half of it into my mouth, chewed, swallowed, and took a sip of the hot delicious coffee. At that early hour of the morning I was the only person in the office. It gives me time to get an early start, sign off on stuff that was possibly left over from the night before, and check my e-mails. As I sat there looking over some papers and signing them I heard the sound of footsteps approaching. I looked up and saw Harvey, the porter. He's always in early on a regular basis. He was making his early morning rounds of emptying wastebaskets. He had left his big porter's cart at the entrance to the area that I am in charge of.

"Good morning Harvey," I said to him pleasantly as he emptied the wastebasket at the desk next to mine, depositing it's contents in a big plastic bag to be put in his big cart when he was done with all the other wastebaskets.

"Good morning Mr. Griffin," Harvey replied and smiled at me. "Beautiful day isn't it Sir?"

"Yeah, it sure is at that," I said and popped the second half of my cereal bar into my mouth.

When Harvey got to my desk I moved out of his way so he could get to the wastebasket under it.

"Always here early eh Mr. Griffin?" the porter asked me.

"Yes I am," I said with a smile. "Lots of work to be done Harvey."

Harvey emptied my wastebasket and continued on his way as I resumed working and sipping my coffee. Could Harvey be the person who kidnapped me? Perhaps he and the young guy at the coffee shop were in cahoots to nab my ass. Shit, I was starting to suspect everybody, even Harvey the porter. Harvey is one of the kindest and gentlest men I have ever met. He is also married and has two small daughters. Why the fuck would *he* want to kidnap me? But God, then, thinking about the big cart that Harvey wheels around the office I thought how that cart was big enough to house a kidnap victim, even a guy as big as myself... My buddy Paul was the first person to arrive at the office after me that day. The rugged blond guy strolled into the office at eight AM sharp. Dressed in a navy blue pinstriped suit with a red silk tie and black wingtips the guy said good morning to me as he approached his desk, which is right next to mine.

"Good morning," I replied as Paul and I shook hands.

"Ready for another day of hard stress and back breaking money making?" Paul asked me as he shucked off his suit jacket.

"Yeah, I guess so bud," I said to him, took in the sight of his massive chest pressing against his crisp white shirt and turned back to my computer.

As the early morning wore on more people began filing in and sat down behind their desks. I sipped down the last of my now cool cup of coffee and threw the empty cup in my wastebasket.

"Hey Joe, do you have one of those customer loan request forms?" Paul asked me. "I seem to be all out of them."

"Yeah sure," I replied, reaching into my desk drawer and extracting a form for him and holding it out to him. "Make a few copies of it and hold on to them for future use."

"Thanks buddy," Paul said, getting up from his chair.

As Paul went to run the copies I felt the need to urinate setting in. I stood up and left the office, walked down the hallway, to the men's room, and walked in. The bathroom was unoccupied except for me. I strolled up to a urinal, unzipped my suit pants, and...and, *and,*

And that was all I could recall of my last normal day of life. God almighty, it was in the bathroom at work that they had somehow snagged me. As another piece of delicious stir-fried chicken was fed to me I tried like crazy and desperately to recall anything after I had gone to the men's room. As I chewed I recalled smelling something really strange and at the same time trying to get my big cock back into my pants and zip up. *Yes, yes, I remembered now!!* I had finished pissing, was about to pack myself back into my suit pants, and that was when it happened. The bathroom had not been unoccupied, as I had thought it was. Someone must have been hiding in a stall, just waiting for me to come in to take a leak, or even a dump. Someone came up behind me and clamped a chloroform soaked rag over my nose and mouth. I struggled like mad in his strong grasp, trying to use all my strength to pull away from him. But he was a strong fucker; iron like bud, and the smell on the rag was beginning to make me dizzy and disoriented. I slammed him up against a wall but he still managed to hold that rag over my nose and mouth. Then, as I thought about what was happening and remembering having read articles about high-powered executives being abducted for ransom I lost consciousness. As I sipped cold mineral water through a straw I wondered how many of them there were and how they had managed to get me out of a public building unseen, *unseen*. I again thought about Harvey the porter and just how big that supply cart of his was. Well, again, not Harvey, it just couldn't be. But I did know that there were a few of those supply carts in the porter's room. All the kidnappers had to do was disguise themselves as porters, help themselves to a cart, and wait in the bathroom for me. But why me and why make me a sex slave of all things? Fuck, that last question was easy to answer. Their note in the bathroom had explained all that hadn't it? The questions of who my captors were and where I had been taken would most likely not be so easy to answer. After I had sipped down the last of the mineral water a deep voice asked me if I'd had enough to eat. I nodded my head, expecting to be chloroformed. Instead, I heard chairs being pulled close to the one that I was seated on. Then, oh God, then, hands and fingers on my chest, men's fingers squeezing my nipples, my cock and balls being grabbed roughly, squeezed, twisted, and my cock slit poked with fingertips.

"Ohhh fuckkkk," I whispered as they pawed me all over.

I balled my tied hands into fists and my head spun as mouths closed on my nipples and sucked them and sucked them and sucked them some more. A hand holding my hardening eight and a half inch guy began stroking me slowly. I curled my toes back under my socks and leaned my head back. My muscular body broke out in goose bumps as I was slowly and forcefully brought to climax.

"Arrrrrrrhhh, f-*fucking kidnappers,*" I seethed and felt myself getting close, despite having been milked like a cow earlier.

I panted, dripped with sweat, and grunted as my nipples were worked feverishly and my eight and a half inch guy was stroked faster. God almighty, after those two faggots had siphoned me repeatedly earlier, was I really going to cum again so fucking soon???

"Arrrrrrrhhh yeah you fucking guys!! Goddamned faggots!!" I grunted throatily and shot a small spurt of my mess onto my stomach area. "Ohhh yeah, got me shooting my damned load of good stuff again!"

Yeah, I guess I was going to cum again, and so soon again at that bud…

Holy fucks, but these guys had ways of working me over that I never knew before…

But then, a rag soaked in chloroform was pressed over my nose and mouth.

"RRRmmmmmffff!!!" I cried helplessly.

Before passing out I heard the deep voice say "Give him enough to keep him out for the night Otis," and then I was unconscious.

In the next morning's main New York City newspapers an article ran very similarly in all three of the publications on the top of page three that read something as follows:

A young corporate banking executive mysteriously vanished from his place of work in the Wall Street area of Manhattan mid morning yesterday. Joe Griffin, "known as Big Joe to his office buddies" was last seen to be entering the men's room on the floor of the building where he works. His CO-worker, a young man wishing not to be identified was the last person to see Joe Griffin when he excused himself to the men's room. The only evidence that Mr. Griffin was at his desk yesterday morning are the facts that people saw him there, his suit jacket was left on the back of his chair, and that he had indeed excused himself to the men's room. CO-workers describe "Big Joe" as very work oriented and said that he would never just disappear on his own this way. Mr. Griffin's superiors have mentioned the possibility of the young executive having been kidnapped for ransom, but as yet no demands have been made for the young man. Joe Griffin is in his mid twenties. Family members are pleading for the young man's safe return if this is the case.

A picture of Joe Griffin was in the inset of the article along with a police telephone number to call with any information about the young man's whereabouts, adding that all calls would be kept strictly confidential.

"OWWW!!!" I roared in pain as the new hooded guy gave my ass cheeks another hard whack with his round leather paddle. "Fucker, *bastard*, got me hanging me here like a slab of beef in some damned butcher's freezer!!"

The next morning I had come to only to find myself in yet another wretched position. When I came to part of me felt somehow rested, as if I had been asleep a lot of hours, rather than just the wee moments in between being chloroformed. Yet another part of me felt beyond miserable knowing that I was still in the clutches of whoever had abducted me. *And another part of me felt downright awful because of the horrid position I was now in.* I was in the room where I had been lashed to the post and milked like crazy the day before. But this time I was hanging upside down by my very roped up socked ankles. Actually, I was hanging from a large wooden rafter beam in the ceiling. My muscular arms were crossed painfully up behind me and roped tightly together in three places. When you're a guy with arms as big as the ones I have getting them behind you is tough work bud. Mounds of heavy-duty rope were wound around my upper torso and under my pecs to support my massive chest and my thighs were also roped together. My cock and balls hung freely for whatever the latest client wanted to do with them. When I saw him come into the room he was like all the others before him, hooded. Looking at him in my upside down position I was still somehow able to tell that he was not one of the men who had already paid to use me like some cheap prostitute. As I stated earlier, don't ask me how I knew these things, somehow I just knew. He was dressed in jeans, a tee shirt, and work boots. In his hand was a round leather paddle, the paddle that he was using to severely rap my butt with over and over. (And harder and harder I might add.) The way I was hung there and his height seemed just right for him to be able to land square blow after blow to my poor muscular rump.

"ARRRRRRGGGHHH!!!" I snarled angrily as he pummeled my butt cheeks hard a few times in succession.

"Have you been bad?" he asked me teasingly and whacked my ass again and again, the stinging blows echoing in the room as they connected with my cheeks.

Shit, I hadn't even been given any breakfast. He whacked me again three good hard ones and I screamed in agony.

"Have you been a misbehaved executive?" he asked me mockingly and walloped the fuck out of my ass cheeks.

"AYYYYYYYRRRRRR!!!" I screamed, writhing and wriggling on the ropes, involuntarily curling my toes back under my socks.

I guessed that my captors didn't want to feed me and then have me worked over like this so soon afterwards. If I had eaten I would definitely have puked my guts up by now.

"Have you been a naughty office boy?" the hooded guy spanking my ass asked me.

Then, he stepped in close to me, placed a hand on my upper arm, and pushed me, setting me swinging back and forth.

"Ohhh shit!!" I ranted as I swung back and forth.

"Are you vulgar and misbehaved you bad boy?" the guy asked me, sounding like a sadistic fem.

Each time I passed him he reached out and gave my ass cheeks a hard stinging whack with his leather paddle.

"H-hey fucker, you perverted Leather daddy," I gasped, my head arched back as I swung like a pendulum tethered to that damned rope. "J-just how much did whoever they are charge you to give you the privilege of wreaking havoc like this on me?"

In response I received two hard stinging whacks on my ass cheeks as I swung slower with each passing.

"ARRRRRHHH!!!" I seethed and squirmed miserably as he set me swinging again.

By now my hairy butt cheeks were no doubt the colors of a fire engine...

As I swung back and forth he landed blow after horrible blow on my butt cheeks.

"Bad boy, naughty boy," the guy snickered behind his hood and whacked and whacked me.

I lost count of how many times he had whacked the fuck out of my poor ass cheeks, but after a while I found myself in tears, screaming and begging for him to stop rapping and torturing me.

"AYYYYYYRRRRR GOD!!" I roared as he held me in place by my arm and really thrashed my butt cheeks over and over.

"Are you a bad boy?" he asked me and whapped and whapped and whapped my ass cheeks.

I could feel them turning more than crimson as he pummeled me and pummeled me some more.

"Ayyyyyyyyy, you bastard, y-you're the bad boy!!" I seethed as tears rolled out of my eyes and across my sweat soaked forehead. "ARRRRGGGGGGGHHH!!! More than a bad boy, you-you're totally fucked up!!"

"Naughty boy, talks bad," the guy said, sounding like a deranged woman as he whapped me on the ass, the thighs, behind my knees.

"Uhhhrrrrrr!!! N-no way to treat an executive of my caliber..." I grunted miserably.

When he finally stopped paddling me I was shaking uncontrollably as I hung there sweating. My ass cheeks felt like they were on fire and as if they had been turned into mincemeat. I could actually feel them twitching as welts bubbled up on them. The guy ran a hand over them and squeezed them liberally. He seemed to be satisfied with the job he had done on them and on his "bad boy."

"Please man, *no more, please, no more,*" I whimpered through trembling lips.

I could see him smiling maniacally from ear to ear through the mouth slid in his hood. Then, he spit into his hand a few times and reached up to grab my semi hard eight and a half inch guy.

"Ohhh GAWD," I gasped as his saliva soaked hand grasped me and began stroking me. "Ohhh fuck, this is sick man! Beat the tar out of me and then jack me off?"

My head spun and the sounds of squishing filled the area as he slowly stroked me and stroked me and was bringing me up to a good sized boner.

"Ohhh fuck, you bastard, getting close already you sadistic son of a bitch!" I seethed.

"Looks like the naughty boy still hasn't learned his lesson," the guy mused.

He stroked me faster, faster, and then I felt it man, I really felt it.

"Ohhh yeah, you fucker, got me cumming like crazy!" I ranted as I spewed a good-sized load of creamy executive ball juice. "AAARRRRhhh!!!"

As he milked my eight and half inch guy my butt cheeks tingled and the fucker gave them a few hard whacks with his leather paddle at the same time.

"AYYYYYRRRR shit!!" I grunted, as I was cumming and being paddled again at the same time. "Miserable fucker, still tryin' to teach this bad boy a lesson huh?"

When I was done spewing my load he let go of my cock, gave my ass a few last whacks, tied a blindfold on me, and walked out of the room. I could not believe I had just been spanked like some misbehaved child. Fuck that, my dad and mom never spanked me like this guy just did. A few minutes passed and then I heard the door open again. One guy slowly lowered me to the floor as the other guy held me by my arms, guiding me down so that my head would not hit the floor. I was crying, shaking, and panting for breath.

"Put him out for a while," I heard the deep voice say commandingly. "He needs it. That client really worked him hard."

A chloroform soaked rag was pressed over my nose and mouth. I gratefully inhaled it this time, welcoming sleep. I slipped quickly into unconsciousness…

When I came to it was the early part of the afternoon and I was shocked to find myself where I was. I opened my eyes and found that I was sitting behind a couple of large garbage pails in an alley behind the building that the bank I work for is housed in. I was sitting propped against the wall totally out of view of passerby on the sidewalk. I was wearing just my white briefs and brown smelly socks. I looked across from myself and saw my suit pants, my shirt and tie and my shoes piled neatly on the ground. Damn, I had been released I thought with joy, still in a semi stupor of sorts. My butt cheeks were still stinging from the beating they had been given and sitting with them against the concrete made the sting hurt even more. What brought me totally back to consciousness was the fact that two big burly homeless men were squatting at my sides, sucking heartily at my big nipples. One of them had my hard eight and a half inch guy out of my underpants through the fly hole in his hand and was holding it tightly.

"Ohhh G-God," I grunted as I tried to get to my feet. "Wh-what is this shit, fucking hungry homeless guys feeding on *my* man tits?"

"Hold still guy," the hefty homeless man on my left said, placing a big meaty hand on my arm, pushing me back down on my stinging butt cheeks. "Let us finish eating here and then you can be on your merry way."

As he spoke the other homeless dude snickered around my other nipple as he sucked the fuck out of it. His lips twitching against my nipple sent ripples of chills through my very being…

The guy who had spoken to me quickly slurped my other nipple back into his mouth and resumed sucking it. His buddy on my other side slurped and sucked at the nipple he had in his mouth, snickering, seeming to know what that was doing to me. At the same time he slowly stroked my eight and a half inch guy.

"Ohhh God, when will this shit end?" I seethed as I sat there being feasted upon and jacked off.

I wasn't tied up or strapped down this time, but I was too exhausted and too overwrought to do anything to stop the two homeless sleazy guys from doing whatever the fuck they wanted with me. After a good (or bad) twenty minutes or so of really eating the fuck out of my nipples the guy stroking me worked my eight and a half inch guy faster…and faster…and faster…

"Ohhh yeah, fuckers," I grunted, stretching my socked feet out in front of myself.

They slurped harder at my nipples. I got to tell you man, after having my man tits eaten that way for such a length of time they became all numb and tingly feeling in the homeless men's mouths.

"Ohhh yeah, yeah, fucking bastards, eating my damned man tits," I seethed as I shot my load, cumming like gangbusters.

I spewed my mess all over my chest and it dripped down to my now two day old pair of underpants…

"Arrrhhh yeah, of all the blasted things," I gasped. "Being used and abused by homeless men…"

When I was done the two men let my nipples slip out of their mouths. The oversized husky pair stood up at my sides.

"Mmmmmm, real tasty tits that handsome big guy has eh?" the guy who had stroked me off asked his friend as they walked off out of the alley.

"Yeah, sure as shit man, I sure am glad those two big guys from the van dropped him off there for us to use," the other homeless man replied.

"T-two guys from the van?" I blurted, quickly getting to my feet now. "Hey!! Come back here you two, *please!!*"

The two homeless men stopped walking and looked back at me. They were looking at me hungrily as I stood there totally on display in just my briefs and stinking socks, my cock and balls hanging out for all to see. What a sight I must have made at that moment bud. To tell it truthfully I felt all vulnerable and sexy at the same damned time.

"Wh-what two guys from the van?" I asked them. "Can you tell me what they looked like? Do you remember what the van looked like?

What color it was?"

"Well now, all that information is going to cost you handsome," the guy who had stroked me off said with a mean looking leer in his eyes, looking excitedly at my erect and overly sensitized nipples.

"I-I have money in my wallet, if they didn't take it," I said automatically, going for my suit pants.

"Don't want your money handsome guy with the big tits," the other guy said and I gulped hard, knowing full well what they wanted even before it was stated for me. "Tell you what, you just settle back against that wall, let us have at those big fat tits of yours again, maybe, just maybe, get you off again, and we just might tell you what you need to know."

"B-but, you might not tell me," I said, standing there in all my musculature as they approached me.

"Well then, you'll just have to let us gorge your tits and find out won't you?" the guy who had stroked me off said to me mockingly.

In a fast move he reached out and grabbed my semi hard cock…

"Uhhh!!! F-FUCK," I garbled breathlessly.

A few moments later I was again seated on the ground as the two homeless men feasted on my nipples, sucking at them like crazy, biting on them and slurping the fuck out of them to put it plainly.

"Ohhh God," I groaned as the cock hungry guy stroked me again. "F-fuckers, all you pervs just love seeing me shoot my executive load…"

My poor eight and a half inch guy felt beyond sore as it was stroked and choked bud… After almost an hour of heavy duty tit eating and after having been stroked to climax twice more the two homeless men told me what I wanted to know, not that it would help all that much. I stood there listening to the two men, still clad in just my underpants and socks, my eight and a half inch guy still hanging out of my fly hole. I was stinking of sweat and cum dripped freely down my chest. Like I said bud, what a sight I must have made at that moment. The van that I had been brought to the alley in was the size of a moving van. It was dark blue in color. The two men who had carried me into the alley along with my clothes were both big and burly and dressed like construction worker types. Why, why did that prey on my mind so much? Who did I know that resembled what these two homeless guys were describing? One of them was real tall, muscular and extremely handsome. They described him as having dark wavy hair, a square jaw, and dark eyes. The other guy was shorter than the first with light brown hair. He was kind of dopey looking but also pretty well built. He had a round face and light eyes. After giving me the information I thanked the two homeless men. They snidely thanked me for my tasty tits as well and for letting them get me off. The first of the two said that it was real riveting for them to watch a big muscle stud like me shoot his load. After they left the alley I quickly got myself dressed and headed for the nearest police station…

It has been more than a few weeks that I was kidnapped and used as a sex slave of sorts but the police have not come up with any leads whatsoever. Sometimes during the night I dream about being strapped down to a table and having my socked feet licked. Other times I swear I can feel the thrash of a leather paddle against my naked butt as I hang upside down like a slab of beef in a butcher's freezer. I know that I will never find out the identities of the men who kidnapped me. But every so often I find myself in the alley behind the building I work in, stripped of the top portion of my suit, and letting those two homeless men chow on my big nipples, and letting them jack me off…

A Boner Book

About the Author

Christopher Trevor was born in July 1963 and grew up in New York City. As soon as he was old enough to know how he began writing fiction and has been writing gay erotic/fetish stories for the past ten to twelve years at this point. He became an avid reader as well from the time he knew how and reads everything from fiction, to non-fiction to biographies of interesting and unusual people, people who have made a difference or who have paved the way for others. Christopher attributes his writing artistic inspiration to artists such as
Etienne, Tom of Finland, Tagame, The Hun, and most notably Joe T, who Christopher has had the pleasure of speaking with and even meeting over the last few years. Christopher states, "Joe T encouraged me to write about my fetish because I was embarrassed about it at the time. Joe T said that when we are embarrassed about something that makes it even more enticing somehow." Christopher totally agreed and never stopped writing in this genre. Erotic writers who inspired Christopher Trevor were: Tom Shaw (author of "That Day at the Quarry), C.S. White (author of Big

Sur), Larry Townsend (author of countless erotic novels), and Mason Powell (author of the classic story "The Brig.")

Christopher discovered that not only did he enjoy writing erotic tales but that after his first bondage experience he had a genuine flair for it. Writing to erotic oriented magazines about his first bondage experience truly opened the floodgates for Christopher where this style of writing is concerned. Christopher thanks the handsome and muscular "Greg" for that experience way back in time. Christopher took "Creative Writing" courses every semester during his high school years and while other friends of his stopped writing what they loved to write about as time went on Christopher never let a day go by when he didn't write something... "I feel that if I don't write every day I will die," Christopher has said many times over.

Foot fetish stories and all things related; spanking fetish, erotic shaving, muscle bondage, tickle torture, and hardcore stories are just a few of the areas of gay eroticism that Christopher enjoys writing about and inspiring in others as well. As one internet buddy said to Christopher where the black socks fetish is concerned, "Until I started talking with you I never gave a thought to my socks when I got dressed for work in the morning. Now when I pull my dress socks on every morning I get a chill up my spine."

Christopher is proud of the erotic effect he has on people...

Christopher Trevor is also the author of:

The Executive Guide to Foot Fetishism and Office Discipline

    1-887895-36-1

Executive Ties That Bind

    1-887895-37-X

Don't! Stop! That Tickles!

    1-887895-31-0

The Taming of Dominick

    1-887895-45-0

Timmy and The Hong Kong Tailor

    1-887895-30-2

Love, Torture and Redemption

> 1-887895-32-9

Timmys Ticklish Trials

> 978-1-887895-74-3

The Gym Instructor

> 978-1-887895-44-6

Milked

> 978-1-887895-66-8

Erotic Street Blues

> 978-1-887895-97-2

The Abusive Wager

> 978-1-887895-04-0

Terry's Appointment and Other Tickling Stories

> 978-1-934625-08-8

The Military File

> 978-1-934625-21-7

Quirks

> 978-1-934625-24-8

Timmy and the Evil Dr. Vonvellicator

> 978-1-934625-42-2

Blackmail

> 978-1-934625-47-7

Tickled Kink

> 978-1-934625-49-1

Humiliation

> 978-1-934625-58-3

Discipline

> 978-1-934625-07-1

Revenge

978-1-934625-60-6

Taking Liberties

978-1-934625-65-1

A Tribute to Leather

978-1-934625-27-9

Look for them where you bought this book, Amazon.com or TheNazcaPlainsCorp.com.

DON'T!! STOP!!
THAT TICKLES!!

Christopher Trevor

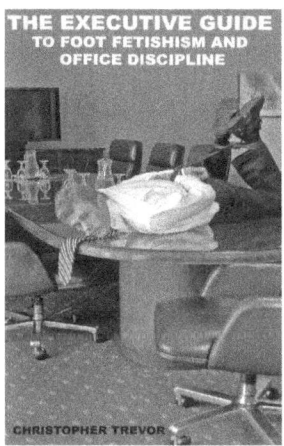

THE EXECUTIVE GUIDE
TO FOOT FETISHISM AND
OFFICE DISCIPLINE

CHRISTOPHER TREVOR

EXECUTIVE TIES
THAT BIND

CHRISTOPHER TREVOR

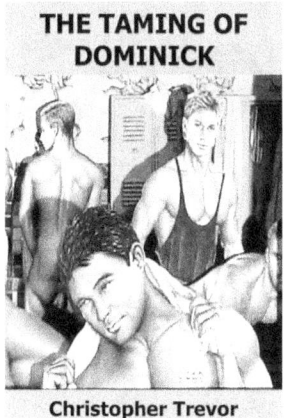

THE TAMING OF
DOMINICK

Christopher Trevor

DISCIPLINE

COMPILED BY
Christopher
Trevor

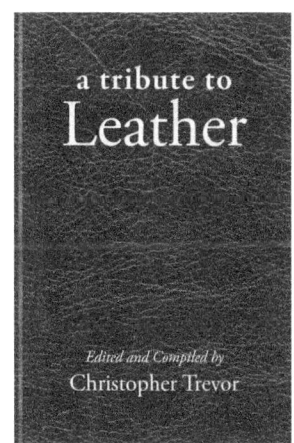

a tribute to
Leather

Edited and Compiled by
Christopher Trevor

TIMMY AND THE EVIL DR. VONVELLICATOR

CHRISTOPHER TREVOR

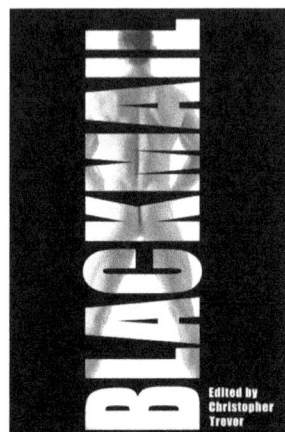

BLACKMAIL

Edited by
Christopher
Trevor

TICKLED KINK

COMPILED BY
CHRISTOPHER TREVOR

HUMILIATION

Christopher
Trevor

Taking Liberties

Christopher Trevor

STRUGGLE

CHRISTOPHER TREVOR

THE JOCK

CHRISTOPHER TREVOR

Love, Torture, and Redemption

Christopher Trevor

Erotic Street Blues

POLICE

Christopher Trevor

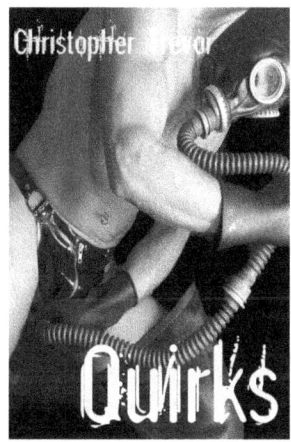

Christopher Trevor

Quirks

REVENGE

CHRISTOPHER TREVOR

TERRY'S APPOINTMENT
AND OTHER SPANKING TALES

CHRISTOPHER TREVOR

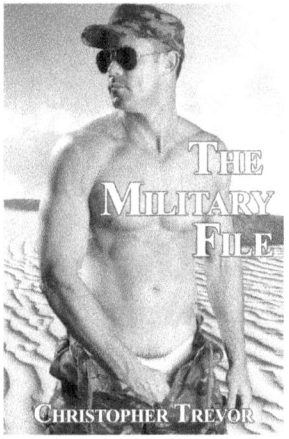

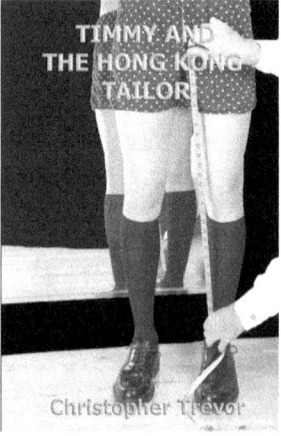

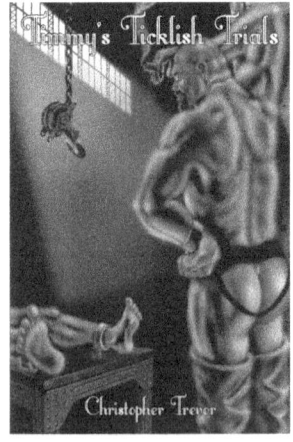